JUNE WRIGHT
Make-Up for Murder

JUNE WRIGHT (1919–2012) made a splash with her 1948 debut, *Murder in the Telephone Exchange*, whose sales that year in her native Australia outstripped even those of the reigning queen of crime, Agatha Christie. Wright went on to publish five more mysteries over the next two decades while at the same time raising six children. When she died in 2012 at the age of 92, her books had been largely forgotten, but recent championing of her work by Stephen Knight, Lucy Sussex, and Derham Groves, combined with reissues of her novels by Dark Passage Books, has restored Wright to her proper place in the pantheon of crime writers.

DR. DERHAM GROVES is a Senior Fellow in the Faculty of Architecture, Building and Planning at the University of Melbourne. In 2008 he curated the exhibition *Murderous Melbourne*, which helped to rekindle interest in June Wright's work.

June Wright with Derham Groves, 2008

Make-Up for Murder

MOTHER PAUL INVESTIGATES

JUNE WRIGHT

Introduction by
DERHAM GROVES

**DARK
PASSAGE**

TO MARCIA AND TONY

 A Dark Passage book
Published by Verse Chorus Press
Portland, Oregon
versechorus.com

Cover design and Dark Passage logo by Mike Reddy
Interior design and layout by Steve Connell Book Design / *steveconnell.net*

Country of manufacture as stated on the last page of this book

Library of Congress Cataloging-in-Publication Data

Names: Wright, June, 1919-2012, author. | Groves, Derham, writer of
    introduction.
Title: Make-up for murder / June Wright ; introduction by Derham Groves.
Description: Portland, Oregon : Dark Passage, 2024. | Series: Mother Paul
    investigates ; [3] | Summary: "Mother Paul, the incomparable
    nun-detective, is faced with her most perplexing case yet when a former
    pupil of the convent school she oversees is murdered at their annual
    reunion"-- Provided by publisher.
Identifiers: LCCN 2024005605 (print) | LCCN 2024005606 (ebook) | ISBN
    9781891241420 (trade paperback) | ISBN 9781891241659 (ebook)
Subjects: LCGFT: Detective and mystery fiction. | Novels.
Classification: LCC PR9619.3.W727 M35 2024 (print) | LCC PR9619.3.W727
    (ebook) | DDC 823/.914--dc23/eng/20240212
LC record available at https://lccn.loc.gov/2024005605
LC ebook record available at https://lccn.loc.gov/2024005606

Contents

Introduction

Rianne May, an Australian singer with a voice like 'golden smoke' who went overseas and made good in London and New York, has returned to her home town of Melbourne to star in her own weekly television show. As its most famous alumna, she has been invited to the annual reunion of former students at Maryhill, a private Catholic secondary school run by nuns. Maisie Ryan, as she was then, cut an insignificant figure during her schooldays, when she was the subject of practical jokes and bullying, but now that she's become the glamorous Rianne May, she has the chance to shine.

And shine she does at the reunion tea party, dominating the room as old grudges and new jealousies swirl around her. Around her table, the worlds of Maryhill and television are intriguingly linked. Sue Berry, Rianne's personal secretary, is another former Maryhill student, as is Lylah Willis, president of the Maryhill Past Students Association and the wife of Sir Hammond Willis, owner of the television station behind *The Rianne May Show*. Lylah is jealous of Rianne, suspecting her husband may be rather more than just the singer's doting boss. She also resents her husband's patronage of her stepsister Carol Frazer, Rianne's make-up artist at the TV studio and another Maryhill alumna.

Then one of Rianne's table companions drops dead, poisoned, just after availing herself of one of the saccharine tablets Rianne offered around when no sugar bowl was on hand. Was Rianne the intended victim? Given that she runs from the scene and subsequently vanishes without trace, she certainly thinks so. And not without reason—she had received a death threat in the post only that morning. Evidently she had been wrong to dismiss it as the kind of crank letter that stars receive all the time.

But who is the murderer? And what has happened to Rianne May? Fortunately the Superior of Maryhill is the redoubtable Mother Paul, who immediately calls for Detective Inspector Savage of Russell Street C.I.B. Mother Paul assisted him—or was it the other way around?—in a previous case, *Faculty of Murder*, and between them they will get to the bottom of the whole business, with Sue Berry as their go-between.

That is the gist of *Make-Up for Murder* (1966) by the Australian crime fiction writer June Wright (1919-2012). It was the last of the six novels June Wright published during her lifetime, following *Murder in the Telephone Exchange* (1948), *So Bad a Death* (1949), *The Devil's Caress* (1952), *Reservation for Murder* (1958), and *Faculty of Murder* (1961). She wrote another novel, *Duck Season Death*, directly after *Reservation for Murder*, but her publisher rejected it, as did another publisher she submitted it to under the pseudonym Dorothy Daniel and with a different title, *The Textbook Detective Story*. *Duck Season Death* was eventually published posthumously in 2015.

Remarkably June wrote these seven crime novels while raising six children, one of them severely disabled; moreover, she received virtually no encouragement to write from her husband, Stewart (1913-1989)—'a formidable bone of contention from way back,' she later mused. Writing was always an uphill battle for June.

June wrote *Make-Up for Murder* in 1964; she signed a memorandum of agreement with John Long in March 1965; and they published the book in February 1966. It was the last of her three books featuring the Catholic nun detective, Mother Paul, all set in Melbourne, June's home town. The Catholic Church certainly moved Mother Paul around a lot, though, considering she was such a capable and talented nun. In *Reservation for Murder* she was the Rectoress of Kilcomoden, a hostel for 'business girls'; in *Faculty of Murder* she was the Warden of Brigid Moore Hall, a residential college for female students at the University of Melbourne; and in *Make-Up for Murder* she is the Superior of Maryhill College, a Catholic secondary school for girls from well-to-do backgrounds. June tended to model

Loreto Mandeville Hall in Toorak, the model for Maryhill in *Make-Up for Murder*

her settings on real places—Frank Tate House and St. Mary's Hall, respectively, in the first two Mother Paul novels—so I suspect she modelled Maryhill on her own school, Loreto Mandeville Hall, in the affluent Melbourne suburb of Toorak. 'Maryhill' and 'Mandeville' even sound alike!

June chose female-specific settings like these, I believe, because they allowed her to depict the worst kinds of catty behaviour among women, something she enjoyed doing and was very good at. It did not go unnoticed: a review of *Make-Up for Murder* (11 August 1966) by R.S.N. that I found in her scrapbook of news clippings accurately stated, 'The envy and jealousy among the women characters, their pride, and scheming, give the authoress occasion to develop a study of these defects, as she weaves a story that holds interest to the last page.' Perhaps the cattiness of the women rings so true in June's novels because she had seen it—nay, participated in it—herself at Loreto Mandeville Hall, where 'many of the pupils had surnames well-known in the specialised medical world of Collins Street and the legal ghetto of the Owen Dixon building at the other end of town,' she recalled in her unpublished memoir. 'Others featured on billboards outside big building projects. One name was that of a Papal count, another a baronet. But their offspring seemed harmless enough; some even a little dull mentally.' Meow!

The poisoning at the Reunion Day tea party in honour of TV star Rianne May reminded me of the poisoning of Heather Badcock at a fete hosted by the movie star Marina Gregg in Agatha Christie's *The Mirror Crack'd from Side to Side*. Published in 1962, four years before *Make-Up for Murder*, it very possibly influenced June Wright, who was a big fan of Christie (and always very proud that she had outsold the Queen of Mystery in Australia in 1948, when her first novel, *Murder in the Telephone Exchange*, came out). In terms of its quality as a mystery, *Make-Up for Murder* is my least favourite Mother Paul novel—partly due to the influence of Christie, but also because there is not enough of the cunning nun for my liking. She is just a voice at the other end of the telephone for large parts of the story (there is a good reason for this, but to explain it here would be to give too much away). On the other hand, from a pop culture perspective, *Make-Up for Murder* is my favourite Mother Paul novel, because it is about television—a subject I have written far too much about over the years.

Television was introduced in Australia in 1956 and remained a national obsession for a decade. Virtually all aspects of everyday life fell under its spell, including even Australian crime fiction, although not to the extent that I might have expected. Besides *Make-Up for Murder*, I know of only three Australian examples of television-themed crime fiction from that era. *The Cold Dark Hours* (1958) by Alan G. Yates, who wrote hardboiled thrillers under the name Carter Brown, concerns an advertising agency executive who devises an ad campaign to sell defective television sets. Marc Brody, the protagonist of a series of thrillers (1955-1960) by the writer and newspaperman William (Bill) H. Williams, is a newspaper crime reporter until 1956 but then becomes 'TV's on-the-spot crime reporter.' And *Who Dies for Me?* (1962) by the underrated crime fiction writer Sidney H. Courtier was about a sinister organisation that secretly watched people using tiny television cameras inside their light globes.

TV sets were prohibitively expensive in Australia in 1956. Not everyone could afford one, let alone two. Watching TV in those days was therefore a social activity for most people, involving a group of people huddled around a household's one TV set, their eyes all glued to the 17- or (if they were lucky) 21-inch black-and-white screen in the corner of the lounge room. Many people worried that watching television would ruin their eyesight, so they usually watched in semi-darkness as if at the cinema, believing this would help. June and Stewart Wright could not afford to buy a TV set in 1956, either; their daughter Rosemary remembers them all visiting a relative to watch the televised opening ceremony of the 1956 Olympic Games in Melbourne. That would have meant seven members of the Wright family (their severely disabled son was living in a home by then) plus however many relatives there were, all watching one TV set.

Since June was familiar with TV-watching etiquette, she included some of these little rituals in *Make-Up for Murder*. When a special edition of *The Rianne May Show* is screened, appealing for information about her whereabouts, Mother Paul has the convent's one TV set moved into the school recreation room so the senior students can also watch it. She tells one of the girls to turn off the overhead lights and 'just leave one of the wall brackets.' Observing all this, Sue Berry recalls that when she was at the school, 'it had been the radio blaring or someone thumping on the piano' in the recreation room. 'Now they all sat in a silent circle, in the semi-darkness, watching a small screen.' Everyone is so engrossed that they don't even notice an intruder entering the recreation room through a window. 'From the back of the darkened room came a high, quavering voice of one of the girls: "Mother Paul! There's a strange man in the room!"' June cleverly used the way people watched television in those days to provide cover for the intruder, but current readers might find it hard to understand how so many people could miss such a thing if they did not know how mesmerizing people found television back then or that they used to watch it in virtual darkness.

Make-Up for Murder contains many details about the production side of television, some of which June Wright possibly observed for herself. When she was promoting her latest book, *Reservation for Murder*, in February 1959, she appeared on the popular TV show *Tell the Truth*, hosted by quizmaster Danny Webb on HSV-7 in Melbourne. The show's format entailed three celebrity panellists interviewing three ordinary people to discover which one of them was actually the person they all claimed to be. 'I met my two fellow conspirators before the show started, and they memorised as much information about me as I could feed them,' June remembered. 'Their role was the more difficult as they had to sound completely convincing, while all I had to do was answer truthfully the questions put to me.' After June and her two imposters had taken their places in a sort of courtroom dock, Webb read out June's affidavit:

> I, June Wright, am the mother of six children, including twins, and this keeps me fairly busy most of the time. But over the last few years, I have developed a rather profitable hobby in writing detective fiction. I am the author of such blood-curdling works as *Murder in the Telephone Exchange*, *So Bad a Death*, and *The Devil's Caress*. My fourth novel, *Reservation for Murder*, was published just before Christmas.

The three panellists then asked the three "June Wrights" questions designed to draw out the real one. 'My fellow players were remarkable, rattling off answers to the most searching questions—one even reciting the names of her alleged six children without a stammer,' June recalled. When her turn came, she made sure she answered any questions about books and writing hesitantly. 'Is Ellery Queen a man or a woman?' one panellist asked. 'Now, I knew the name was a pseudonym for a pair of male collaborators,' June wrote later, 'but I would have given myself away if I had said that, so I ummed and erred but without telling a lie until he gave up and asked the next question.' Finally, the panellists settled on the woman with the six fictitious children as her. 'Would the real June Wright please stand up,' Webb then commanded. 'I rose slowly to my feet and, averting my embarrassed gaze, I gave the Ellery Queen interlocutor a nod of apology—to which he replied with a shake of his fist,' said June.

Even though her television appearance was nine years before the publication of *Make-Up for Murder*, June had already decided to write a book set in the world of television, telling her daughter Rosemary that she had agreed to appear on the show, despite being very nervous, because it was research. Certainly, *Make-Up for Murder* provides a colourful and detailed picture of the fledging television industry in Australia. Sir Hammond Willis—aka 'the Big Man'—is cut from the same cloth as the real-life Australian media baron Sir Frank Packer, who owned two TV stations, TCN-9 in Sydney and GTV-9 in Melbourne. While not as bombastic as Sir Frank, Sir Hammond is similarly outspoken to everyone, regardless of who they are: 'I never allow anyone to stop me once I have made up my mind to anything, Inspector,' he tells the police. Since the United States was the mecca of television, many Australian TV stations sent their leading on-screen personalities and behind-the-scenes technicians there to learn the business: this is the case with Carol Frazer, Rianne's make-up artist and Lylah Willis's stepsister, in *Make-Up for Murder*. 'I understand [Sir Hammond Willis] paid for Carol's trip to America and her training over there and has also made himself responsible for the rent of her flat,' Sue Berry tells Inspector Savage. 'Perhaps he feels somewhat to blame for the rift between Lylah and Carol.' Oh yeah, I bet he did! The gossip and scandal surrounding many of those on television were, of course, bonus entertainment for the viewing public. Roger Petrie, the producer-director of *The Rianne May Show*, belongs 'to that stratum of society which provided material for the TV magazine gossip columnists,' notes Sue with a degree of pride and envy. Rianne has a few skeletons in the closet herself, as you will soon discover. No spoilers!

The Wrights finally bought a TV set in 1957. 'It was an Astor with a big wooden cabinet,' recalled their son Stephen. Naturally, June loved to watch crime shows on television, her favourite being the American private detective series *77 Sunset Strip*, starring Efrem Zimbalist Jr, which was broadcast in Australia on GTV-9. Her husband Stewart never missed *In Melbourne Tonight* (popularly known as *IMT*), the nightly live variety show hosted by the irreverent and funny Graham Kennedy, also on Channel 9. In July 1964, Stewart lost his job and suffered a debilitating nervous breakdown. 'He worked grudgingly at any job during the day and watched television for hours at night,' June recalled years later. '*In Melbourne Tonight* was his particular solace—the public persona of Graham Kennedy, successful, witty, and well-groomed, became the ideal of everything he wanted to be. His perceptions were unreal—and infinitely sad!'

June's particular solace in those years, on the other hand, was writing *Make-Up for Murder*. I suspect that *IMT* and Mother Paul merged in June's imagination and she based Rianne May on *IMT*'s most adored singer, Elaine McKenna. 'June certainly would have used the *IMT* personnel for her novel,' Rosemary Wright told me. Elaine was Catholic, like Rianne, and would have had to be better and fight harder to achieve success in Melbourne in those days than Protestants would—something that would have earned a big tick from June.

Like Elaine McKenna, Rianne starts her showbusiness career by singing on radio talent shows in Melbourne, which leads to a small part in a variety show at the Tivoli theatre, followed by minor roles in a couple of touring musicals, then regular nightclub work that allows her to earn enough money to travel to London. Over there, her first triumph is an appearance at the London Palladium, followed by cabaret spots, parts in West End musicals, and guest spots on television in London and New York. In the real-life case of Elaine, television came at just the right time. The producer of *IMT*, Tom Miller, chose the bubbly 19-year-old receptionist to sing on the show over sixty other hopefuls. 'In the late Fifties and Sixties, every man and boy was in love with her,' said Bert Newton, Graham Kennedy's talented straight man and a close colleague of Elaine's. In 1960, she made a well-publicised whirlwind tour to Amsterdam and London, then in 1961 moved to Los Angeles, where she was hailed as 'the second Mary Martin.' She performed with comedian Bob Newhart on television and in night-

clubs around the country, such as the Chi Chi Club in Palm Springs and the Chase Hotel in St. Louis. Elaine came back to Australia periodically to visit family and make guest appearances on *IMT* and other TV shows before returning home for good in 1968. Rianne, like Elaine, has broad appeal and—most importantly for Australian TV audiences of the era—the common touch. The press described Elaine as 'Melbourne's girl next door,' while in *Make-Up for Murder* Rianne is dubbed 'the girl who is everything to everyone.'

Elaine McKenna and Bob Newhart in Australian slouch hats, hamming it up of *The Bob Newhart Show* (1961).

(*Left*) The dust jacket of the original edition of *Make-Up for Murder* by William Randell, depicting the TV singer Rianne May; (*right*) the photography of Rosemary Wright (*standing*) with June publicising *Faculty of Murder*. Randell based Rianne's face on Rosemary's.

The dust jacket of the first edition of *Make-Up for Murder* features an image of Rianne by the prolific British illustrator William Randell. Stephen Wright has recalled disapproving comments by his father, Stewart, 'about the risqué nature of the dust jacket art.' Rianne is shown in a low-cut dress, singing her heart out, surrounded by backstage television paraphernalia. Randell also designed the less bosomy dust jacket for June's previous Mother Paul mystery, *Faculty of Murder*; in total he created hundreds of dust jackets for an impressive stable of crime writers, including fellow Australians Jon Cleary, Charlotte Jay, and Shane Martin (George Johnston), as well as international luminaries such as Rex Stout, Ruth Rendell, Ellis Peters, and Mignon G. Eberhart, the latter a skilled exponent of the 'Had I but known' school of mystery writing and one of June's favourite authors. Randell used Rosemary's face in a photograph of her and June taken in 1961 to publicise *Faculty of Murder* as the basis for Rianne's face on the dust jacket of *Make-Up for Murder*. 'During Swot Vac of that year, an interviewer visited Mother at home for publicity and took my photo for the dust cover,' Rosemary told me. Curiously, she looks like a young Elaine McKenna in this photo.

In her round-up review of new crime fiction in the *Coventry Evening Telegraph* (17 February 1966) Susan Hill observes that 'detective stories are moving farther and farther into the regions of the thriller. International gangs, major robberies, political undertones, and foreign countries all rear their ugly heads. The quiet, English closed-circle whodunit is becoming a rarity. Pity. But *Make-Up for Murder* by June Wright (John Long, 16s.) stays near the old style, although there is an underground political force in which people are mixed up.' Hill is referring to a secretive group called the Servants of Peace that June introduces late in her novel, who are attempting to recruit people in the entertainment industry to spread their ideas about how to cure "this poor, sick world." Their inclusion may baffle a few readers, so allow me to provide some context. June wrote *Make-Up for Murder* during the era of the Cold War, when anti-Communist hysteria was at its peak, and seems to have closely followed events in the preceding decade in the USA, when the House Un-American Activities Committee conducted public witch hunts against liberal and left-wing figures in the American film and television industry, accusing them of making movies and TV shows that spread soft Communist propaganda.

In *Make-Up for Murder*, an emissary of the Servants of Peace tries to recruit Sue Berry by arguing that 'the poor duped public think they know what they want, but only people like you and me, pre-pared to serve others, know what is good for them.' Sue is puzzled and vaguely alarmed, but the penny only drops after it is explained to her that 'it's not servants they aim to be. It's masters, dictators . . .' 'You mean they're some kind of political movement—out for power? Like Hitler?' she naively asks, and then concludes, 'That was why the leaders of such groups wanted to get hold of actors, authors, and politicians, knowing that the ordinary man in the street could swallow doctrines without realising. It was horrible.'

I must say that of all of June's female protagonists, Sue is by far the least capable and self-assured. She is no Maggie Byrnes from *Murder in the Telephone Exchange*, that's for sure! However, given the stress that June was under at home due to Stewart's depression, on top of the responsibility of raising six children, it does not surprise me that the heroine of *Make-Up for Murder* struggled to cope sometimes too.

Make-Up for Murder was the last Mother Paul mystery, although June Wright did not plan it to be—she started writing a fourth, set in the little coastal town of Queenscliff, sixty kilometres as the crow flies south of Melbourne. She summarised the plot in her memoir as follows: Mother Paul is holidaying at Santa Casa, a holiday retreat for nuns, when a body is discovered on the beach— a blonde woman stabbed to death while sunbathing. She was the cranky mother of two toddlers, unhappily married to a leading Melbourne barrister, and had been staying in one of the holiday cabins next to Santa Casa. It seems the murderer mistook her for a similar looking but decidedly dumber and less genteel blonde who is staying in another of the holiday cabins. This woman's husband, a notorious criminal, had been planning to join her but is murdered in some drug-related payback before he can get there. Mother Paul finds his body washed up on the beach as she enjoys an early morning stroll along the beach while the younger nuns are swimming. In the meantime, Mother Paul has befriended the nanny of the dead woman's two toddlers—a student doing a vacation

Santa Casa, Queenscliff, the setting for June Wright's uncompleted fourth Mother Paul novel.

job who has long, slim legs and long, silky hair like the British model Jean Shrimpton; she is also a part-time vocalist with the rock group that plays at a pub in the nearby town. The story is told from the nanny's perspective, June recalled, 'with Mother Paul sorting out the clues from the red herrings—of which there are shoals, including the occupants of the other cabins, a sinister local fisherman, a cache of uncut diamonds thrown overboard from a passing ship, and more drugs.' While the plot seems complicated, it also sounds interesting.

June had a winner in Mother Paul and could have kept writing mysteries featuring the wise old nun detective for the rest of her literary life. Robert Sommerville, her London agent, certainly wanted more and kept enquiring about the progress of the fourth Mother Paul book. 'We like your character so much that we are prepared to do all we can to get you published,' he said. However, raising six children and coping with Stewart's mental breakdown, which compelled June to find work outside the home to earn a regular income, meant the task of finishing the book was beyond her. 'Finally, the agent wrote no more, and I sadly buried my stillborn literary baby in a file marked "Memorabilia" before turning to face the pain of the present,' June wrote. She still hoped that once her husband got back on his feet, she might go back to writing books again, 'having remained ever unhappily aware of the half-written story hidden in my desk.' But even though he did, June was through with writing. Sadly, she did not live to see the publication of *Duck Season Death* and the reprinting of her other six crime novels by Dark Passage. But she did get to see *Murderous Melbourne: A Celebration of Australian Crime Fiction and Place* (2008), the exhibition I curated at the Baillieu Library, the University of Melbourne, which championed her work. 'She was eighty-nine years of age, and her words were no longer flowing freely,' June's son Patrick recalled. 'With tears in her eyes and patting her chest, she managed to say to Derham, "Thank you, thank you from my heart."'

June Wright's legacy lives on, and with the reprinting of *Make-Up for Murder* all her mysteries are now out there to read once again.

DERHAM GROVES

MAKE-UP FOR MURDER

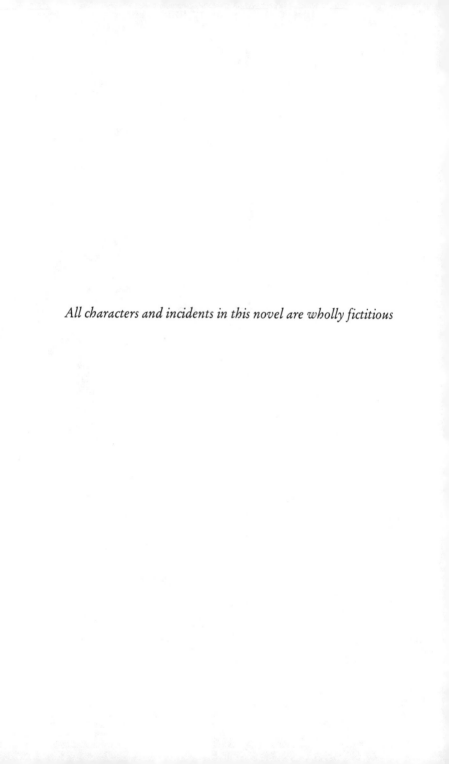

All characters and incidents in this novel are wholly fictitious

I

As Sue read the deckle-edged card, a nostalgic smile tilted the corners
of her mouth. For a few moments she was back again at school. She
could see Mother Paul's soft eyes which nonetheless could unveil
your most closely guarded secrets. She could hear the gentle voice
which was never raised in anger. She remembered with poignant
intensity the nun's understanding sympathy when Sue's mother had
died, and again when her father had remarried.

Sue sighed even as she remembered: undoubtedly her days as a
boarder at Maryhill had been the happiest of her life. She had been
bolstered by a sense of security and belonging she had never known
since. There had been no room for her in the house which her father
shared with his second wife, and her brother had gone to live in a
remote part of the country with his family . . . but she shied away from
recalling the desolate years which had followed her leaving Maryhill
and deliberately turned her attention once more to the invitation card.

*The Mother Superior and community of Maryhill request
the pleasure of Miss Suzanne Berry's company at the Annual
Reunion of Past Students, to be held in the school hall on
Sunday, June 4th, at 3 p.m.*

The word 'over' was written in ink across the right-hand corner.
On the back a short note ran: *Could you possibly persuade Rianne
May to come too? Everyone would be so thrilled!*

Sue placed the card back on the pile of mail she had been sorting through at the table which she used as a desk. Rianne, clad in

skin-tight leather slacks and a shaggy black pullover, was pacing the room as she poured out a non-stop commentary on her show the previous night, alternating between despair and exuberance, fulsomeness and vituperation.

It hadn't taken Sue Berry long to learn that one of her duties as secretary to a famous television star was to be a patient audience to such scenes, that they were Rianne's way of getting rid of tension following a performance. Provided they didn't interfere with her employer's monologue, Sue was always able to continue with whatever secretarial tasks she happened to be engaged on, such as opening the stack of fan letters Rianne's chauffeur had brought up from the television studios.

When Sue had found her own name she had opened the envelope eagerly, strangely happy that someone knew she was back in Australia and cared enough to get in touch with her. Nor had she been disappointed by its contents. It would be pleasant to see Mother Paul and Maryhill again.

But she was dubious about the request that Rianne should also attend the reunion. Somehow Sue could not visualise Rianne sipping tea and talking over faraway schooldays. She could not, in actual fact, remember much about Rianne at Maryhill. Then her name had been Maisie Ryan. The preposterous switching of Christian and surname—to Rianne May—had taken place abroad.

Sue's mental picture of the old Maisie Ryan was of someone who always looked shabbily old-fashioned, who was rudely rebellious and ostracised by her fellow students for no other apparent reason than that she was different from them and only shone—and then none too brightly—at school concerts and in the Dramatic Society. As children, none of them could appreciate that Rianne's aggressiveness stemmed from loneliness and a deep-seated inferiority complex because she was without parents. Both had been killed abruptly in a car accident, leaving Rianne in the care of a widowed grandmother who found the spirited child altogether too much for her.

On the plane which brought them from England, Rianne had told Sue something of the story of her early struggles to establish herself in some branch of show business after the death of her grandmother, how she had started in Melbourne by winning a radio amateur hour contest which led to a small part in a Tivoli variety show. This had been followed by tours in a minor role with a couple of musicals and some night-club work which gave her enough money to go to Europe. In London, life at first had been even more of a struggle, but her almost frenetic determination to succeed, coupled with a definite talent, had pushed her slowly up the ladder. Her first triumph came with an appearance at the Palladium, an occasion she never tired of describing. Gradually she received more offers than she had ever dreamed of—cabaret spots, parts in West End musicals and finally television shows. In this latter medium she became particularly successful, building up a reputation which spread to the United States. Several times she had been flown to New York for special guest appearances in television programmes. Then for some reason—probably to show herself as a local girl made good—she suddenly accepted an Australian offer for her own national television show. *The Rianne May Show.*

Rianne came to a swiftly posed standstill on the somewhat grimy lambswool hearth-rug. The furnished flat, which was the property of the television company, had housed other stars under contract and their imprints were everywhere—cigarette burns in the bathroom, darkened cushions and ring marks on the furniture.

'Help me, Sue!' appealed Rianne, using a voice once described by a word-happy critic as filled with golden smoke. I desperately need an objective opinion of the show. No excuses, no pretty pretences-just plain, honest-to-goodness facts.'

Sue surreptitiously slit another envelope and waited for Rianne to start pacing again. Once she would have been deceived by such an appeal into thinking that a real person was about to take over from the temperamental artiste. There were times when Sue felt fond of Rianne and enjoyed working for her, but there were other occasions when she wondered how much longer she could stand the artificiality of her personality and that of the world in which she moved. It was then that she had to remind herself of what she owed to Rianne—how she still might be stuck in that dreadful little Earls Court room, with its sink and gas ring curtained off in one corner, with the four walls crowding in upon her, had not Rianne recognised her that desperate day at Australia House.

Rianne, splendid in a summer suit by Givenchy and surrounded by officials, press and television representatives with their numerous hangers-on, had been there for publicity shots on the eve of her departure for Australia. Over the flowers, the toy Koala bear someone had presented to her, and the crowding admiring heads, her restless, laughing eyes had fallen upon Sue.

Rianne's gaze had become arrested, the laughter fading from her eyes as a lovely enquiring look came into them, she was still wearing the expression when a photographer called for another pose. By the time the flashlights had finished exploding she must have become intrigued as to where she had seen Sue. One of the hangers-on was sent to ask Sue to wait as Miss May wanted to speak to her—she was so certain she knew her. Sue admitted that they had been at the same school many years ago in Melbourne. And the hanger-on said 'Really!' and swallowed his Adam's apple in astonishment that the same school could have produced two such dissimilar girls.

It was quite some time before Rianne could get to Sue. In fact, Sue wouldn't have been surprised had her curiosity evaporated. Later she came to realise that the value Rianne automatically placed on the personal touch in her contacts with her fans had been in her favour. Within minutes of their meeting and the other's extravagant ejaculations, Sue found herself telling Rianne how she had left home with little more than her fare to England, and the high hopes she had had of being able to find secretarial jobs in London in between making tours round England and on the Continent. But things hadn't worked out the way she had planned and now she was flat broke, homesick for the land of her birth and was hoping someone at Australia House might be able to help her to get there again.

When Rianne, almost immediately and just as casually as proposing a stroll down the Strand, suggested she accompany her as her personal secretary, all expenses paid plus a liberal salary, Sue was so overcome that the hanger-on was ordered to fetch a glass of water. Within five whirling, bewildering, hectic days Sue found herself back in Australia once more. It had been difficult to believe her sudden and unexpected good fortune. Her debt to Rianne could never be paid, Rianne's extravagant flights of fancy must always be forgiven.

'When I gave up a perfectly good contract in England to come out here,' Rianne was saying fretfully, 'I didn't know I was expected to compere a Sunday School concert—which is what last night's show amounted to. You can't tell me Australian viewers are as naive as all that. The material I was supposed to handle! Answer me seriously, Sue darling—has the studio no other script writer but that gauche young man who always breaks into perspiration when he comes near me? What's his name? Johnnie something or other.'

'Bexhill,' Sue supplied the surname before she added dryly: 'But I thought you were pleased with his stuff. Last night after the show you told him—'

'Last night, last night!' Rianne snapped her fingers impatiently. 'Whoever remembers what one said last night. It's what one thinks in the cold light of dawn that counts. I simply shudder to think what the critics must be writing right now!'

'They are more likely being taken to task by their editors for using too many superlatives,' said Sue soothingly. 'Anyway, what do you care? You always say the public matters more than the critics, that the public is the proper judge of your work. I heard that the studio switchboard was jammed for over two hours after you closed.'

'Of course it was jammed,' snapped Rianne, flinging off for another leopard prowl round the room. 'You aren't suggesting a show of mine was a flop, are you? Though heaven knows it could have been with Eric making ten-second signals at me all the time. What a floor manager!'

Sue did not say anything, even though Rianne had allowed a couple of cues to run over time during the programme. Eric Watts, the floor manager, did his own share of moaning to her about Rianne, whom he claimed to have known in British television before he migrated to Australia. He was always dropping patronising hints that it was, in fact, due to his good offices that she ever reached stardom. Another of Sue's duties was that of a buffer between the studio staff and Rianne. The only times she ever found the job pleasant was when the grave and handsome Roger Petrie, director-producer of the *Rianne May Show*, solicited her help in getting Rianne to rehearsals on time and asked her advice about ways to encourage the star's co-operation.

Rianne's tirade was dwindling into a series of petty complaints. Very soon now, as Sue knew from experience, she would find something else to galvanise her into fresh energy. Then she would forget all about the scene she had put on and the wild and ridiculous statements she had made.

The clock, chiming softly on the mantelpiece, provided the necessary diversion. Rianne let out a small shriek of alarm. 'Is that the time? I shall be horribly late. Sue, you should have reminded me about my appointment with Hammond instead of wasting time talking about the show. I simply loathe post mortems, anyway.'

A flash of the famous smile to show Sue she was both rebuked and forgiven, then Rianne was gone from the room in one of her swift and graceful camera exits that always gave viewers the breathless feeling that she had vanished into thin air before their eyes.

With a rueful expression, Sue went back to sorting the letters. There had been only two editions of the *Rianne May Show*, but the fan mail was gratifyingly large even discounting the usual number of begging letters and appeals for charity appearances. It was an indication of Rianne's amazingly wide attraction that letters came from all sorts of viewers from all walks of life.

Some were written in the round, unformed writing of adolescents, others in the thin quavering strokes of old people. There were proposals of marriage and other proposals less respectable. 'The Girl Who Is Everything To Everyone' was the headline a national magazine had given Rianne May and the letters seemed to endorse that.

Suddenly the wry smile on Sue's face vanished. On a sheet of plain bond paper in capital letters were pasted words made up from newsprint which read startlingly:

— YOU ARE GOING TO DIE SOON RIANNE MAY

After a moment of bewildered shock Sue picked up the envelope in which the letter had come. Pasted-on words also formed the address of the television studio. It was a simple device. Rianne's name and that of the channel had been printed a hundred times in the press during the last weeks.

Sue gazed from letter to envelope, not unduly disturbed. Where there were celebrities there were bound to be cranks. A threatening letter was practically on a par with an erotic one. She wondered if she should withhold it from Rianne, as the studio had instructed her to do with any obscene or worrying letters.

Rianne's voice, calling from the bedroom, cut across her thoughts. 'Tell Ted to bring the car round, will you, Sue? I shouldn't be more than five minutes.'

Sue started up, still clutching the anonymous letter. She wondered briefly if she should show it to Ted, who as well as being Rianne's chauffeur also acted as her bodyguard, specially appointed from the television company's security staff by no less a person than the governing director himself, Sir Hammond Willis. But if she did that, Ted might have to make an official report about the letter to Sir Hammond, and Rianne might be annoyed that she hadn't been consulted first. Deciding to give the whole matter more consideration Sue put the letter in its envelope and slid it under her typewriter.

Sue found Ted sitting in the kitchen, reading a paper-backed Western, his peaked cap and leather gloves on the table beside him. He was a tall, well-built man with a thick thatch of fair hair and a shy grin which combined to give him a boyish, disarming appearance. His slow way of speaking and his unfailing good humour sometimes irritated Sue, but there were other times when she found his quietness comforting and a relief from Rianne's histrionics. He was always do-ing little things for her, too, and just then had the coffee percolator bubbling on the stove.

'Miss May wants the car ready in five minutes,' Sue said, looking round vaguely for a coffee cup. She hadn't quite had time to acquaint herself with the contents of the flat. When Ted handed her one from the first cupboard he opened, she said: 'You know this kitchen better than I do. How long have you been playing nursemaid to television personalities?'

Besides his other duties, Ted seemed a kind of general handy-man who went with the flat and had a room downstairs next to the garage. 'I've only just got the job,' he confessed sheepishly. 'I was hoping it wouldn't be too apparent.'

Sue frowned. 'Oh, then you wouldn't—' she broke off, and pretended to look for the sugar bowl. A bottle of saccharine tablets belonging to Rianne, who had to watch her figure, was lying on the table and she shook one into her cup.

'I wouldn't what?' prompted Ted.

'You wouldn't be able to give me any tips on how to cope with the star temperament,' finished Sue smoothly. 'Better get going, Ted, or Rianne will be putting on another performance—for your benefit.'

'Aren't you coming to the studio then?'

'No, I'm working here today. You're to take Rianne into town for a luncheon engagement with Sir Hammond. He will see that she gets to the studio, and you can pick her up later from there.'

Ted collected his cap and gloves. 'That makes it the third time this week that she's had lunch with the Big Man,' he observed dispassionately.

'Well, at least she can't come to any harm while she's with him,' said Sue without thinking. She caught Ted looking at her from the back door, a startled expression in his usually enigmatic eyes, and was glad that the telephone started to ring in the living-room. Putting down her coffee, she hastened to answer it. Rianne hated a telephone to be left ringing for any length of time.

'Is that Miss Suzanne Berry?' asked a hesitant voice. 'Miss May's secretary?'

'Yes, Sue Berry speaking. Who is that?'

'You may not remember me, Sue, but my name is Eunice Hurley, Eunice Rawson that was. We were at Maryhill at the same time, but of course you were a little younger. I used to go around with Lylah Frazer and Janet Gordon. Lylah married Sir Hammond Willis, you know, and Janet is a doctor.'

'I remember you vaguely,' replied Sue guardedly. 'And I met Lylah again recently at a reception the studio held for Rianne May.'

'Dear Maisie! So difficult to remember she's Rianne May now. Such a spectacular creature! So different from what she was at school . . . how we used to laugh at those clothes and that awful old grandmother who looked after her. It all seems incredible, doesn't it?'

Sue said nothing. She felt something was behind all this. She thought of the invitation from Maryhill and the words on the back of the card even as Eunice spoke again. 'Sue, did you get notice of the reunion? Yes, of course, you did. How silly of me! Janet and Moya and I sent out the cards together and I recall addressing yours care of the studio. They're both members of our Past Students' Association.' She seemed unable to stop herself talking. 'I'm the secretary, Moya is the treasurer and I daresay you know Lylah is president. She's simply marvellous. Works so hard on any number of charities. How she manages to fit them all in, I can't imagine! A day a week for the Red Cross, another visiting Wesburn Repatriation Hospital, then the spastic children at—'

'Is it in connection with the invitation to the reunion that you rang me?' asked Sue, stemming the list of Lady Willis's charitable activities.

'Well, not your invitation precisely.' Mrs Hurley's voice was shaded with anxiety. 'I suppose you noticed what was written on the back?'

'About getting Rianne to put in an appearance? I haven't mentioned the matter to her yet, but I doubt if she'll be able to make it. She has a pretty tight programme.'

'Oh, I know. In fact, I've been thinking perhaps you'd better not tell her about the invitation, Sue. She might feel she ought to come, Maryhill being her old school and all that. We'd hate her to feel under any obligation.'

'Who's we?' asked Sue bluntly. She had the distinct feeling that she was being manoeuvred into something and didn't like it. 'Who wrote that message on the back of my invitation?'

'Well, I did, actually,' admitted Mrs Hurley. 'Janet was insistent— don't you recall how forceful she always was at school? Well, she's worse now. Oh, dear, I shouldn't say things like that. It's unkind. Being a doctor I suppose she has to be strong-minded . . .' her voice trailed off helplessly.

Sue laughed. 'Not only am I beginning to place you, Eunice, but I'm also beginning to see daylight. The committee wants Rianne to attend the reunion, but you yourself are afraid of what Lylah Willis is going to say.'

Sue had a momentary vivid impression of Eunice way back in school, forever hovering about Lylah, desperately anxious to please— poor sycophantic Eunice who only made Lylah more autocratic and spiteful. Things had not changed, it seemed, despite the intervening years and marriage. Eunice still held Lylah in awe.

'Oh, Sue!' expostulated Mrs Hurley. 'But I have to admit that's about the strength of it. You see, I feel a sort of loyalty to Lylah.

She's been awfully good to me. I haven't had an easy life, Sue. I'm a widow now, with a daughter going to Maryhill. She's the same age as Lylah's girl, Sandra. They're such chums, Jilly and Sandra. It would be awful if . . . I don't know why I'm telling you all this. Perhaps I shouldn't have rung. Perhaps Lylah won't mind. After all, men of Sir Hammond's age often, so I'm told . . .' She gave her nervous giggle.

'What have you been told?'

'Nothing. Absolutely nothing. Please forget what I said. Just a slip of the tongue.'

'Very well, Eunice. But I will tell Rianne about the Maryhill invitation. It will be up to her whether she attends or not. Goodbye.' She replaced the receiver on an anguished 'Oh, but Sue—'

Rianne dashed in for help in zipping a dress. 'Ring Ham and tell him I'll be a bit late, will you, Sue? Who was that you were talking to?'

Sue picked up the receiver again. 'An old school-friend of yours, Eunice Rawson. Eunice Hurley now, I gather.'

'School-friend? I had no friends at school. You know all that jazz about the happiest days of your life? I was never more thoroughly miserable. The inferiority complex all those ghastly little snobs gave me! What did she want?'

Sue found the invitation. 'Read the message on the back,' she said as she dialled through to Sir Hammond Willis's secretary. 'He's already left,' she informed Rianne a moment later, 'but Miss Mills will get a message through to the Clover Room.'

Rianne was turning the card over and over, a faint, not very pleasant smile on her mobile mouth. 'Well, well! The old school! How perfectly charming! Shall I go to the reunion, Sue?'

'They would love to see you,' Sue replied quietly.

'They would? Awkward, self-conscious Maisie Ryan with the darned stockings and the parish school accent?'

'You're not Maisie Ryan now. You're the talented and famous Rianne May. Eunice called you spectacular. It's only natural that Maryhill wants to claim a distinguished past pupil.'

'Well, I don't want to be claimed,' said Rianne peevishly, her mood changing quickly as it always did. 'I've got enough to do without providing a sideshow for a lot of sycophants. Neither do I want to be reminded of what I was like at school. I've spent too many years trying to forget it. I've got a tough position to maintain and I'm not having my confidence sapped.'

'Very well, Rianne,' said Sue, taking the invitation out of her hand. 'I'll write a note of excuse.' She turned away, adding in an offhand voice: 'Lylah Willis will be pleased you're not going.'

'Lylah Willis? What do you mean? I thought you said it was Eunice someone or other.'

'Eunice Hurley, a friend of Lylah's, trying to stop me from telling you about the reunion.'

A gleam of mischief shone in Rianne's expressive eyes. 'You mean it would annoy Lylah if I did attend? Maybe I'll go then.'

'Is it only to annoy Lylah that you're lunching with her husband for the third time this week?' asked Sue boldly.

Rianne chuckled. 'Prim little Sue. Do you disapprove? A girl has to get on, you know. Besides the poor man needs some companionship.'

'His wife doesn't understand him, I suppose,' said Sue dryly.

'That she doesn't. She thinks he's a lecher if he looks at any woman twice. That pretty child in the make-up room, Carol somebody, was telling me.'

'Carol Frazer, Lylah's stepsister.'

'Yes, that's right. She used to live with them until Lylah took the notion that Ham was about to look a third time at Carol. She practically threw the poor girl into the street.'

'The story I heard was that Sir Hammond sent Carol to the States with a cost-plus-expense account to learn studio make-up and get experience. Then when she came back she decided to get a flat on her own.'

'Lylah wouldn't have her back. She made the filthiest innuendos.'

'I wouldn't feel too sorry for Carol,' suggested Sue. 'She's got a good job even in spite of Lylah, and a good boy-friend in Johnnie Bexhill, your perspiring script writer, to protect her from third glances from Sir Hammond, should she need protection, which I doubt.'

'Every girl needs protection,' Rianne said in an unexpectedly soft voice, and made another of her swift exits.

Sue looked after her sharply. There had been something in Rianne's comment that struck her as being genuine—a faint crack of insecurity in the brilliant façade? Though Rianne had spoken often and amusingly about her love affairs, only one half of which Sue believed, knowing how Rianne delighted in trying to shock her, she had never before even hinted at any personal need. There had been something curiously lost and wistful about Rianne when she had said 'Every girl needs protection,' and for the first time Sue thought that the threatening note might be serious.

On impulse she picked up the anonymous letter from its hiding place under the typewriter and went to Rianne's room. 'Here's another piece of correspondence I think you should see!' she said gravely.

Rianne flapped a hand at her in the mirror. 'Don't worry me now.' She applied street make-up with a swift skilful hand and placed a hat, which could only have been an original model, on her honey blonde hair in one unerring movement. 'My stole, will you, Sue?'

It lay across the big, satin-covered bed. Sue crossed the room. 'This letter I want you to look at, Rianne. It's probably a hoax, but I don't like the sound of it just the same.'

'If it's someone after money, just tear it up.' Rianne draped the mink about her shoulders and swivelled round to see the effect.

'Here! Read it for yourself.'

Rianne had begun working her fingers into gloves, but she bent forward to read the letter Sue was holding out. The abstracted expression left her eyes to be replaced by one of sheer terror. Her lovely clear-cut face seemed to grow rigid.

'A hoax, of course,' she said after a moment, and gave a shaky little laugh. 'The sort of thing people in my position have to put up with. Why did you show it to me, Sue? A good secretary wouldn't worry me with such things.' She sounded suddenly irritable, and unattractive lines appeared around her mouth and eyes.

'I'm sorry, Rianne. I wouldn't have shown it to you if I'd known you weren't going to take it seriously.'

'Of course I don't regard it seriously. Don't be a fool, Sue! I've had abusive letters before now.'

'All the same,' Sue said quietly, 'perhaps we ought to consult someone about it—perhaps inform the police.'

'The police!' exclaimed Rianne shrilly, her well-modulated voice unrecognizable. 'Are you out of your mind?'

Sue stood her ground. 'I don't think so. Why should you object to telling the police that someone has made an anonymous threat against you? It's the sensible thing to do.'

'Because I don't want to, that's why,' Rianne snapped. 'The . . . the publicity might kill the show. They'd only think it a hoax, anyway. And that's all it is, so get rid of the beastly thing and don't mention it again to me. Or to anyone else.'

Sue eyed her unhappily. 'What about allowing me to tell Ted Brown? He's supposed to be your bodyguard. He might have some suggestions.'

'He'd be clueless, you know that. I can scarcely get a word out of him. It must have been his brawn which got him the job, not his brains. And, anyway, as I've told you, there's absolutely nothing to get worked up about. In fact, I wish you'd stop nagging about it. I'm as jumpy as a cat now. Go and mix a drink and do something useful, instead of showing me filthy anonymous letters. You really must learn to be more discriminating, Sue, otherwise I might have to —' Suddenly she caught sight of herself in the mirror. 'And just look at my face now that you've upset me, damn you!'

Sue walked steadily back to the living-room, trying to control her anger. She opened the cocktail cabinet and mixed Rianne's drink slowly and methodically, thinking all the time of that squalid Earls Court room where she had spent so many lonely and miserable hours. But even empty loneliness was preferable to being insulted! Her colour was still high and her lips compressed when presently Rianne swept in, apparently fully recovered from her bout of nerves.

'Darling,' she drawled enchantingly, scooping up her glass. Her face was fresh and young again, her smile dazzling. 'I was a bitch talking to you like that. Please forgive?'

'Yes, of course,' replied Sue stiffly.

'You sound cross still. But I did warn you, Sue, didn't I? Remember that day in London? I told you I could be bitchy and never to take too much notice of what I said. It's the life I have to lead. You know that, don't you, Sue? You won't go walking out on me, will you?'

Again that real note in her voice, thought Sue. She responded to it instantly. 'No, I won't do that, Rianne. I'll never forget what you did for me that day.' She hesitated and then said with some difficulty: 'If there's any way I can help you, apart from being your secretary, you know you can trust me.'

'Of course, darling! You do a fabulous job, too. What more help could I possibly need? I haven't a care in my mind. I'm on top of the world.' Tossing off the remainder of her drink, Rianne handed the glass to Sue and rearranged her stole. 'I feel better. 'Bye now.' And she went off quickly, banging the front door behind her.

Sue waited until the company's Mercedes went purring down the street. Then with a slight shrug she crossed to her table, held the anonymous letter over an ashtray, flicked a lighter and watched it dissolve into ashes.

2

'Have you ever seen the old hall so packed for a reunion before!' exclaimed a committee member of the Maryhill Past Students' Association. Sue smiled agreement and turned in her chair to look down at the familiar room, a swift succession of assemblies, examinations, concerts and school dances passing through her mind. The committee, which consisted of about a dozen women voted from a cross-section of age groups, sat at a special table set upon the stage, the long blue velvet curtains of which had been drawn back. The main body of past students had divided themselves into friendly groups at the numerous smaller tables already set for afternoon tea in the auditorium. Superficially it was a charming scene—snowy cloths, big bowls of late blooming chrysanthemums and everyone dressed at the peak of fashion to outvie each other. Laughter intermingled with chatter produced a steady, treble-keyed roar, a cacophony of sound which was exhilarating.

Smiles and waves were directed up at Sue and she nodded in recognition, even though some of the faces she found difficult to associate with the right names. Some looked too plain or too pretty or not the right age to be the girls she had once known. The contradictory changes wrought by the years were strangely disturbing. Only the nuns seemed to have remained the same, even those who had appeared quite ancient to Sue when she was a plain, quiet child in Mother Paul's infant class. They glided from table to table, smiling happily at old pupils and remembering names from twenty and even thirty years back.

'Is that Father Maher down there?' someone demanded incredulously, as though following Sue's train of thought. 'I thought he'd be dead by now. He must be a hundred.'

The doddery old priest in the rusty cassock who had been Maryhill's chaplain for years was enjoying being made a fuss of at one of the tables. Sue recalled the cottage where he lived and how it had been strictly out of bounds to the students. Known as the Priest's House, it was situated in the pine grove at one end of Maryhill's extensive grounds.

'There are quite a number of visiting nuns here today, too,' another girl observed. 'They admitted quite openly they only came to see Rianne May. Aren't they pets?'

'If she deigns to appear,' remarked the president irritably. 'Are you sure she's coming, Sue? We have got a meeting to hold and M.P.S.A. business to attend to, you know.'

'She'll be here, Lylah,' Sue replied quietly, surveying the handsome, arrogant face. 'Some people dropped in at the flat which delayed her dressing. She said she would follow me shortly.'

'As her secretary you should have got rid of them and seen to it that she was on time,' retorted Lady Willis, shuffling papers about importantly. 'Though I daresay she would have found some other excuse to be late so that she could make a solo entrance.'

Sue chose to ignore the remark. She even had it in her to feel a certain sympathy with Lylah if she really felt Rianne was taking her husband away from her.

There were disquieting undercurrents at the table on the stage which contrasted sharply with the gaiety and friendliness of the atmosphere below. Sue attributed them to the gossip which linked Rianne's name with that of Sir Hammond Willis. Lylah Willis was not a subtle woman. Rich, proud and insensitive, it would not occur to her to make any attempt to hide her dislike of those women favoured by her husband's attentions. She still displayed an open animosity towards her young stepsister, Carol, for having gained Sir Hammond's indulgent protection, which Carol reciprocated to the full. Lylah had even been known to keep a sharp eye on her schooldays' friend and close companion, Eunice Hurley, though Sir Hammond had stated in unequivocal terms what he thought of Mrs Hurley's helpless, clinging ways and her attempts to be the understanding friend of the family.

Anyone not well acquainted with the formidable Lady Willis would have wondered how the twittering Eunice had ever come to be made secretary to the Association, but those more familiar with the president's domineering ways would have guessed that she had to have an acquiescent secretary who would not only give her the necessary support against dissidents like Dr Janet Gordon, the vice-president, but could also be browbeaten into doing most of the donkey work.

At the moment, with about as much finesse as a bulldozer, Lylah Willis was making it clear that Rianne May was not going to be allowed to dominate a meeting chaired by that well-known charity organiser and professional do-gooder, Lady Lylah Willis. 'Frankly,' she proclaimed, sweeping her imperious gaze round the table, 'I can't see what there is about the woman that makes everyone rave.'

'Can't see or won't see?' murmured Carol in Sue's ear.

'Then you are unique, Lylah,' said Janet Gordon forthrightly. 'Rianne has already achieved a tremendous following here, to say nothing of the fans she made in England and America.'

Ignoring Dr Gordon, Lylah Willis fixed a compelling eye on her secretary. 'In my opinion people are like sheep when it comes to television personalities.'

'You're so right, Lylah,' agreed Eunice obediently, adjusting the fur cape Lady Willis had given her when stoles first came into fashion.

'And not only when it comes to television stars,' remarked Carol. 'Do tell us what you thought of Rianne's show, Eunice.'

Mrs Hurley glanced timidly at Lady Willis. 'Well, er, I thought it was quite nice. But some of the jokes were . . .' she wrinkled her nose meaningfully. 'And Rianne's gowns were rather . . .' she coughed delicately.

'The whole programme was fatuous and in very poor taste,' stated Lylah roundly. 'I've warned Hammond the Australian public won't stand for it.'

'What rubbish you talk, Lylah!' said Dr Gordon briskly. 'I am no television enthusiast, but at least I'm honest enough to admit Rianne has a talent and personality above the usual run. She certainly held my attention the other night and as a rule I abominate variety shows.'

The treasurer of the Association, who had been engrossed in studying her report and balance sheet in earnest preparation for the general meeting, looked up for the first time. 'Are you talking about Rianne May? I simply adore her—on the screen, that is. I'm just thrilled at the prospect of actually meeting her. Can anyone remember what she was like at school? She was before my time.'

'Quite insignificant, my dear Moya!' answered Lady Willis, smiling graciously on another member of her committee whom she was in the process of shaping into use by little favours and marks of attention. 'Gauche and spotty, with the hem of her tunic always unstitched at the back.'

'A description that could fit almost any schoolgirl,' declared Janet Gordon flatly. 'You've obviously very little real recollection of what school was like, Lylah.'

'I can recall enough to say Maisie Ryan was no credit to Maryhill,' snapped Lady Willis. 'And she still isn't.'

'We used to laugh at her in Junior School,' remarked Carol thoughtfully. 'Do you remember some of the tricks we played on her, Sue? And how unpopular she was?' She waved a slim hand with long gleaming nails at the hall. 'And now everyone is bending over backwards to meet her!'

'Mass hysteria!' exclaimed Lylah Willis angrily. 'I think I'll call the meeting to order now. I understand that Moya has something of importance to tell us.'

Eunice put a hand on her arm. 'No, wait a little longer. Some of the boarders have formed a guard of honour in the drive. It would be a pity to spoil things. Please, Lylah.'

Lady Willis's high colour became richer. 'I never heard such nonsense! Anyone would think Maisie Ryan was royalty.'

'Your daughter is going to present the bouquet,' Carol informed her with relish.

'Sandra? I want her to have nothing to do with that woman. Is this some of your customary mismanagement, Eunice?'

Mrs Hurley rolled an appealing eye round the table. 'I thought we should . . . that is, we thought it might be nice—'

'Eunice's girl is in the guard, too,' said someone, with misguided staunchness. 'But we all firmly agreed that the president's daughter should be the one to present the flowers. It seemed more fitting.'

'Oh, did you? And why wasn't I consulted?'

'For the very obvious reason that we knew you'd make a jealous fuss, Lylah,' Janet Gordon told her calmly. 'As you are about to do now.'

'I think Rianne must be arriving,' Sue intervened. 'I can hear the children clapping.'

An excited buzzing filled the hall. Chairs were scraped back as everyone rose and stared expectantly at the main doors. Several women even clambered on to chairs to obtain a better view.

Rianne May entered the hall hand in hand with Mother Paul, the present superior of Maryhill. She was throwing a laughing glance over her shoulder at the guard of honour which had broken up into excited groups of schoolgirls begging for autographs. She spoke a word to the nun beside her, dropped her face caressingly against the huge bouquet across her arm, then looked up in surprised delight at her assembled alumni.

Sue felt a reluctant smile on her face. No one but Rianne could have managed an entrance at once so poised and yet so innocent and shy. It was a superb piece of acting.

Mother Paul beckoned the nuns who were scattered about the hall. They came forward and an expression of sweet respect slipped easily on to Rianne's enchanting face as she spoke to each one of them. She stood among them, laughing and talking and completely charming them.

'She looks like some beautiful, brilliant bird surrounded by magpies,' uttered Eunice in misty-toned accents. 'Isn't she just too wonderful?'

'Don't be an emotional fool, Eunice, please,' said Lady Willis witheringly. 'Go and bring her here. That is the duty of a secretary. Tell her this is a meeting of the M.P.S.A. not a Rianne May Fan Club.'

'I'll fetch her,' offered Sue.

The nuns broke away, and now Rianne was being besieged by throngs of past students all anxious to claim her attention. Sue moved through the shifting, craning groups trying to catch her eye.

'Why, it's little Suzanne Berry!' exclaimed a gentle voice nearby. 'Dear me! So many years!'

'Mother Paul!' said Sue, and leaned forward to receive a swift soft kiss on either cheek.

A pair of mild, yet penetrating blue eyes scanned her affectionately. Sue remembered how impossible it had always been to meet that gaze after childish peccadillos. 'You're looking very well, dear child. Maisie—oh, dear, I must remember to say Rianne—tells us you're working as her secretary. Now she has changed almost out of recognition—so odd!'

'Why odd?' asked Sue, laughing because Mother Paul herself hadn't changed and this made her feel warm and secure.

'One expects something recognisable from youth. She is quite a different person.'

'She's been leading a somewhat different life since Maryhill.'

Mother Paul looked about her. 'Yes, so many changes, and not only Rianne. So sad and just a little . . . frightening!'

'Frightening?' repeated Sue sharply.

The nun nodded pensively. 'To see new lines and unfamiliar expressions on faces one knew so well once. The outside world must be a very trying place to live in.'

'It is,' agreed Sue, smiling again, 'but there are compensations.'

'There would need to be,' declared Mother Paul simply, turning as someone touched her arm.

'Would you excuse me, Mother Paul?' asked Eunice Hurley, straightening her hat which had been knocked askew over her anxious face. 'Sue, Lylah is simply furious. Do get hold of Rianne and bring her to the committee table. Oh dear, I shouldn't have let the girls talk me into sending that invitation.'

'Let me try,' suggested Mother Paul. 'And you go and tell the laysisters to start serving afternoon tea, Eunice. That will make everyone sit down again.'

The clamouring crowd about Rianne fell away as the nun gently pushed her way through, holding Sue's arm in a light clasp.

'Oh, there you are, Sue darling!' cried Rianne gaily. 'I thought you had completely forsaken me.'

'I've been trying to get through your fans. There's a special place waiting for you at the committee table, Rianne. Will you come now? Afternoon tea is about to be served.'

'Tea? How scrumptious! Mother Paul, do come with us.' Rianne kissed her hand to the subsiding crowd. 'Oh, how wonderful this is, to see all the girls again and the dear old school! Do you know, Mother Paul, when I was struggling to make a name in London I used to think of Maryhill. It was my inspiration.'

'If Maryhill has helped in your success, then Maryhill has been rewarded, Rianne,' said the nun gently.

'How sweet of you to put it like that. Tell me, have you seen my show? Sue, the nuns must have a television set. Make a note to mention it to the studio tomorrow. And get Publicity to inform the Press that I shall be presenting it in person.'

Mother Paul looked apologetic. 'The M.P.S.A. has already given us one out of their Amenities Fund.'

'Perhaps you could make some other sort of presentation, Rianne,' said Sue quickly. 'I believe there are various other funds. I'll have a word with Moya.'

All eyes followed Rianne as she approached the stage, taking in the superbly simple Paris clothes she wore that somehow made everyone else look either dowdy or overdressed.

'I'll have to leave you now, Rianne,' said Mother Paul, smiling. 'It's time for the boarders' tea, too. Anyway, you'll all want to talk about old times.'

'This way, Rianne!' Sue led the way to the table where Lylah Willis was the only one who had remained seated.

'You certainly took your time, Sue,' Lylah said cuttingly. 'How do you do, Maisie!'

'Lulu, darling! How delightful to see you again!'

Janet Gordon let out a guffaw. 'Lulu! I'd forgotten we used to call you that, Lylah!' She thrust a hand at Rianne. 'Well, I'm not going to risk calling you Maisie if it's going to remind you of a nickname for me.'

'Dr Janet Gordon, Rianne,' said Sue quietly, seeing that Lylah had no intention of unbending.

Rianne allowed her hand to be touched briefly. 'I remember you, Janet. You were sports captain and used to make my life miserable because I was absolutely hopeless at all games.'

'I'm sorry you haven't more pleasant memories,' replied Janet stiffly.

'Oh, that's not the only memory I have of you,' Rianne positively cooed.

'This is Moya Curran,' put in Sue hastily. 'You had left when Moya came to Maryhill, Rianne. She's responsible for the accounts.'

'Oh, Miss May!' breathed Moya. 'We are so honoured to have you here today. I think your programme is the best thing we've ever had on television.'

'But how charming of you, Moya!' Rianne's smile was pure enchantment.

'This is your place, Rianne, next to Carol. You know her, of course.'

'Hi there, honey!' said Carol chippily, and was rewarded with a blank cursory glance. Rianne was skilled at squashing familiarity and Carol's job at the studios did not entitle her to be flippant in public.

Sue hurriedly introduced the other committee members to Rianne, wishing fervently that she hadn't shown the invitation to Rianne. It was obvious that Rianne was going to enjoy getting her own back for all the rejection of her schooldays. It was threatening to be an explosive meeting altogether, and Sue trembled. Eunice Hurley came up, followed by two young girls dressed in the uniform white frocks Maryhill boarders wore on special occasions.

'Welcome, Rianne May!' cried Eunice, regarding her with a tremulous smile. 'This is indeed a red-letter day in the annals of Maryhill, isn't it, girls? But I don't suppose you remember me. How can you after all these years and the wonderful, glamorous life you have been leading.'

'Stop being fulsome and sit down,' commanded Lady Willis impatiently. 'Eunice Hurley, the secretary of our Association, Rianne. Whether you remember her or not is immaterial.'

'But of course I remember Eunice,' said Rianne. 'She was always allowing you to push her around, even at school.'

Lady Willis said: 'Indeed!' in frosty tones, while Mrs Hurley smiled weakly. 'I don't . . . I mean, Lylah doesn't—'

Rianne placed the sheaf of hot-house gladioli on the table and smiled radiantly at the watching faces. 'I was always being pushed around, too. But the difference between Eunice and myself was that I wasn't willing to be pushed. I never got anything out of it, unlike Eunice. Which is why, when I left Maryhill, I made up my mind to do the pushing instead.'

'Well, I must say we're very entertained at being told the secret of your success, Rianne,' said Lylah coldly. 'I suppose we shall be seeing it in print soon. After all, we've read everything else there is to know about you—at what Paris fashion house you buy your clothes, your special diet, the men in your life and all the other fascinating details.'

'Don't you dislike your life being made so public?' asked Janet abruptly.

'Dislike it?' Rianne opened her eyes wide. 'Why should I? I have nothing to hide.'

'Everyone has something to hide, something they're ashamed of,' insisted Janet.

'I bet I could find a thing or two you'd prefer no one to know,' said Carol provokingly to Rianne. 'You'd be surprised at the gossip you hear in the make-up room.'

'Not in the least, my dear,' answered Rianne gently, turning amused eyes on the younger girl. 'I overheard an interesting titbit only the other day about you.'

Carol tried to match her nonchalance, but her small white teeth were clamped together as she smiled. 'How fortunate then that, like you, Rianne, my life is an open book.'

'Oh, I would never tell tales,' replied the other reassuringly. Her wide smiling eyes went deliberately to Lylah's stony face and then on to Janet Gordon. 'Any more than I ever told tales at school.'

Eunice broke nervously into the taut atmosphere. 'Here are Jillian and Sandra!' She beckoned the two girls who had been standing aside, exchanging giggles and secret looks. 'They are going to wait at our table. Rianne, I'd like you to meet my little girl. She has been so excited all day at the prospect. Jilly, darling!'

The girl came forward reluctantly and muttered something inarticulate. Eunice slid an arm about her. 'She's shy,' she confided to Rianne fondly. 'And this is Sandra—isn't she like Lylah?'

Lady Willis said haughtily: 'What's this about waiting at the table? Since when have Maryhill girls been trained to be waitresses?'

Sandra tossed her head. 'Oh, Mummy,' she said pettishly. 'You know we always do on Reunion Day. We like it.'

'Well, if that's the case, go along and start serving then,' said Lylah coldly.

One of the committee women invited Rianne to tell of her climb to fame, and she was kept busy answering questions from all sides. Sue heaved a little sigh of relief and relaxed in her chair. Rianne was in her element. They were all vastly entertained and the peals of merriment from the committee table brought others up to listen, too. The two small schoolgirls carried cups of tea and plates of cakes and sandwiches to and fro.

'Excuse me a moment, Miss May,' someone interrupted. 'Would someone pass the sugar down this end, please?'

'There isn't any,' said Sue. 'Jillian, would you mind getting a bowl from another table?'

'Sugar?' exclaimed Rianne gaily. 'You girls don't want to use that. Think of the calories. Here, have one of my saccharine tablets.'

'I really must go on your special diet, Rianne,' said Eunice with a regretful sigh.

'There's no time like the present,' suggested Rianne, shaking the contents of her little bottle into the centre of the table.

'Oh, may I? Who else wants their tea sweetened? Lylah?'

'No, thank you,' Lylah said primly.

'Never mind about the sugar,' Sue said to Jillian. 'It seems we're all off to the Rianne May diet.'

Rianne sipped her tea and waved away a dish of proffered cakes. 'Now, where was I?'

'Outside the B.B.C. trying to decide whether to try vamping or table-thumping.'

'Oh, yes—well, my dears, I did neither. Because just at that moment who should drive up in his Daimler—'

Sue only half-listened. She had heard the story before of Rianne's meeting with the head of B.B.C. Light Entertainment and dozens of other meetings with famous names.

Instead, she looked round the hall reflectively, wrapped in memories. Suddenly her eye was caught by a movement at the opposite end of the table. Janet Gordon was bending over Moya, who appeared to have fainted. It took a little time for the commotion about them to subside and then everyone was looking at Janet and asking what was wrong.

'Moya's ill, I think,' Janet said in a puzzled voice. 'She seems to have collapsed. I can't hold her, she's a dead weight. Would you all move back please, and I'll put her on the floor.'

There were exclamations of alarm and offers of help.

No one afterwards could ever remember precisely what happened in those moments when Moya Curran died!

3

Later, when Sue gave her account of what happened to the police and Mother Paul, they made her repeat it over and over again. She told them how Janet had laid Moya on the floor and someone had found a cushion to put under her head. How, in the confusion, the bowl of flowers on the table had been knocked over and the cloth dragged askew as they all pressed forward. She remembered how Janet Gordon had felt for Moya's heartbeat and how she had bent right over her to try mouth to mouth resuscitation, how she herself had caught that odd smell which she foolishly thought must have been one of the almond cakes they had had for afternoon tea . . .

Janet's face was queer and white when she finally lifted her head. She got up slowly and looked round the circle of women. Her voice was hoarse. 'She's dead! I think she's been poisoned.' She picked up one cup and then another and sniffed them gingerly.

Silent and aghast, they stared at the body on the floor. That was what it was now—a body. Not Moya Curran, treasurer of the Maryhill Past Students' Association. They watched Janet close the staring eyes and loosen the clenched hands. Then she pushed the tea things to one side and, dragging the cloth from the table, spread it over the body. Someone started to weep hysterically and was soon joined by others. Sue heard Eunice, who was witlessly rearranging the scattered flowers back into their bowl, exclaim over and over: 'Oh, it's awful, it's just too awful!'

'Stop it!' cried Janet. 'Stop it at once, the lot of you! Eunice, I'll slap you in a moment. Where's Mother Paul? Sandra, please go and find her.'

Then Rianne spoke. She, too, had risen and was incongruously holding the sheaf of gladioli across her arm again. She looked round the distorted, frightened faces which were only a reflection of the fear in her own. 'Who did it?' she demanded harshly. 'Which one of you? It was meant for me, wasn't it?'

Sue seized her arm. 'Be quiet, Rianne! You don't know what you're saying.'

Rianne tried to shake herself free. 'I'm not a fool. I know someone is trying to kill me. It wasn't meant for Moya. It was me.' Her voice was ugly with fear.

She pushed Sue away roughly and backed through the surrounding crowd.

'Rianne!' cried Sue. 'Rianne!' She tried to follow her. 'Let me through, please.' But the throngs that had parted for Rianne had closed the gap. By the time Sue reached the doors of the hall, there was no sign of Rianne.

She was about to run outside when Mother Paul hailed her from the passage. 'Sue, what has happened? I'm told that Moya Curran has had an accident.'

'She's dead,' Sue told her baldly, too worried about Rianne and shocked at the events to prevaricate or to wonder at the effect her abruptness might have.

Mother Paul looked at her blankly for a moment. Then the noise from the hall reached her and at once she was her old, calm self. She said: 'I must go and quieten them. Sue, look at me.' She took the girl's chin in one of her gentle hands and examined her face intently.

Sue stared back humbly.

'Yes, yours is the one face that hasn't changed,' the nun said softly.

'Mother Paul, Rianne has gone. She's absolutely terrified and I'm worried. She said it was meant for her, not Moya. There was a letter threatening her life.'

'Don't try and explain anything yet,' said the nun. 'Listen closely, Sue. I want you to go to the telephone—you remember where it is, don't you? Ring Police Headquarters at Russell Street and ask for Inspector Savage. Give him my name—oh, dear, it's Sunday afternoon, he probably won't be there. Well then, insist that they get in touch with him somehow and have them send him here at once—Inspector Robert Savage!'

She gave Sue a push in the direction of the telephone, and then walked resolutely into the Assembly Hall.

From the platform Janet was vainly trying to quell the panic, but, as Lylah Willis was issuing contrary exhortations, the result was chaotic. Seeing a handbell on one of the window sills, Mother Paul picked it up and mounted the dais, ringing it loudly. Something about the formidable black and white figure standing on the Assembly Hall stage, calmly surveying the room, made the years roll back. Here was the voice of authority which must be obeyed. The voices dropped; then, as the nun touched the bell briefly once more, they ceased entirely.

'You may sit down,' said Mother Paul and obediently they sank into chairs, some so carried away by the nun's commanding presence, so grateful to have matters taken in hand, as to place their feet neatly together and fold their hands in their laps. 'Now I want you all to observe complete silence while I make enquiries from your president and committee as to the cause of this disgraceful and uncontrolled behaviour. Then I will make a short statement. Is that clear? Now silence, please.'

She stepped across to the committee table. Janet greeted her with a shaky grin. 'Mother Paul, you're wonderful! They were in an utter panic.'

'I can't say that I blame them,' replied the nun, her eyes on the shrouded figure on the floor. 'An unprecedented thing. Frightening.' She stooped swiftly and lifted the cloth just enough for her eyes alone to see the contorted face. Then she straightened and thoughtfully surveyed the dishevelled table. The eyes of the committee members, now seated around it, watched her tensely.

'Which was Rianne's place, Lylah?' Mother Paul asked then.

'She was sitting next to Carol with Sue Berry on her other side,' replied Lady Willis. Her usually emphatic voice was oddly husky and she cleared her throat nervously. For the first time events had been taken dramatically, tragically, out of her hands and she seemed momentarily at a loss. But as the nun turned to speak to Janet Gordon, suggesting that she ask Sister Celestine to go to Moya's parents to break the news as gently as she could, Lylah recovered herself sufficiently to pack her papers together. 'Since it is apparent there will be no meeting today, I think I will go, if that is in order.'

At once Eunice was on her feet in her sycophantic fashion, muttering in a shocked voice: 'Poor Moya! What a thing to happen—and of course there can be no meeting without her. Who else could understand the balance sheet?'

Mother Paul quietly faced the silent auditorium. 'I want you all to stay for a while, if you would. There seems to be nothing further we can do for Moya except to offer a silent prayer for her, and her family. But it seemed to me to be a case for the police and so I have asked Sue Berry to ring them.'

There were some swift, indrawn breaths, and Eunice Hurley began to sob again. 'I'm so upset,' she whimpered. 'Mother Paul, couldn't I go? I must see Jilly, she is so highly strung, a shock like this might—'

'Jillian and Sandra are with the other boarders. Mother Gabriel is looking after them.'

Lady Willis expostulated: 'But why the police, Mother Paul? Surely you don't believe Janet's premise that Moya has been poisoned? She could have had a heart attack, anything. Sudden death doesn't necessarily mean murder . . . it is iniquitous for us all to be kept here.'

Carol Frazer made an involuntary movement. 'Rianne!' she cried. 'Didn't you hear what she said?'

'You can never take into account what that woman says,' said Lady Willis. 'She is thoroughly irresponsible, always wanting to drag the spotlight on herself . . .'

'What did Rianne say?' Mother Paul asked quietly. She had been glancing from one speaker to the other with bright, alert eyes.

'She said someone was trying to kill her, that Moya was killed in mistake for her. Then she dashed away.'

'That woman would try to steal scenes on her death-bed,' declared Lylah spitefully.

'We heard her say it, too,' put in one of the committee in a scared voice. 'Mother Paul, couldn't we at least move away from . . . from here? I don't think I can stand the sight much longer. It's too awful.'

'My dear, of course. Everyone step forward and Carol and I will draw the curtains. Has Father Maher been sent for?'

'He was in the room when it happened. I think he went to the Chapel. Yes, here he is now!'

Mother Paul went quickly to assist the old priest up the dais steps. Together they disappeared behind the curtains. Everyone waited quietly and it seemed an interminable time before they emerged again. The obedient, but tense, palpable silence in the hall was broken by a gathering murmur as the double doors were opened. 'It's Sue Berry,' announced Carol.

Sue had paused on the threshold, half-turned away from the room, talking to a group of men just outside. Then one of the men separated from the group and followed the girl as she hesitantly led the way through the quiet tables to the steps of the stage. Mother Paul went down to meet them.

The impassive expression on the face of the man behind Sue changed abruptly when he saw the nun. His brows went up quizzically and, though he spoke with deference, there was a note of amusement in his voice. 'Mother Paul!' He took the hand held out to him warmly. 'I thought we might meet again some day.'

'So shocking that it has to be as an accompaniment to violent death,' she returned, gazing up at him trustfully. 'Such a relief you're here, Inspector. It's all very puzzling.'

'You surprise me,' he replied gravely. 'Miss Berry said a woman has been poisoned.'

'Moya Curran, one of our past students. Such a good girl, always very conscientious and hard-working at school. Such an unlikely victim!'

Sue said hesitantly: 'I know Rianne believes—'

'All in good time, child,' interrupted Mother Paul. 'Moya was the victim, whether intended or not. Inspector Savage wants to hear about her first, is that not so, Inspector?'

He nodded. 'Where did this alleged poisoning take place?'

'Up here, during afternoon tea.' Mother Paul indicated the curtains and he followed her up the steps.

A subdued buzz broke out in the room as the curtains folded behind them. Sue re-joined the committee and at once was bombarded with questions.

'I don't know anything,' she replied quietly, 'beyond the fact that the inspector's name is Savage and he seems to know Mother Paul.'

'Where did Rianne go?' asked Carol. 'She was in a terrific flap.'

'Probably Ted—her chauffeur—took her home. She'll be safe enough with him.'

'Do you think she was right, that Moya was poisoned by mistake?'

Sue repeated what Mother Paul had said: 'It's Moya's death the police are here to investigate.'

At that moment Inspector Savage pulled the curtains apart and called out to Sue: 'Would you ask my men to come now, please, Miss Berry?'

They trooped in, stalwart young men with cases and cameras, their faces hard and intent, making a discordant note amongst so much femininity. Mother Paul held the curtains aside for them, and then went to the edge of the stage. Her voice was quite calm, but filled with a great sadness.

'By now you will all have learned of the shocking tragedy that has taken place. Moya Curran has died from poisoning—whether by accident, intent or even her own hand the police are not yet in a position to say. Inspector Savage asks that the committee members and any of you who came near the table to remain behind. The rest may go. This has been a terrible occasion, but I would like to thank you for your co-operation.'

Presently the hall was empty, save for the members of the committee who huddled together on the stage, too stunned now to say a word.

Carol broke the silence. 'Sandra and Jillian were on the stage. Shall I go and get them?'

'Perhaps Sue wouldn't mind fetching them,' suggested Mother Paul smoothly. 'In the boarders' recreation room, Sue. And tell the lay-sisters to start clearing the tables—all but this table, of course.'

'I get the message,' said Carol and tried to laugh. 'Though why Sue should be above suspicion I wouldn't know.'

Eunice Hurley looked at Mother Paul with frightened eyes. 'What does Carol mean? What's going to happen now? I really don't want Jillian mixed up in . . . in anything.' She turned to Lady Willis. 'Lylah, you say something to that policeman. He'll listen to you—people always take notice of what you say.'

'This whole affair is thoroughly disgraceful,' proclaimed Lady Willis roundly. 'I must say I am quite shocked at the attitude you have taken, Mother Paul.'

'What attitude, Lylah?' asked the nun meekly.

'No one here could possibly have had anything to do with Moya's death even if she were poisoned, which I very much doubt.'

Come out of the sand, Lylah,' said Janet impatiently. 'If it was cyanide—and I'm prepared to stake my reputation as a doctor that it was—then someone here today must have administered it. Cyanide acts rapidly. Which means that one of us or someone hanging round the table must have slipped it into Moya's cup only moments before she died. Funny thing, though, I couldn't smell it in her cup.'

'How dare you suggest such a thing, Janet! It's outrageous! Moya must have taken it herself.'

'That could account for my not being able to trace it,' admitted Janet thoughtfully. 'But why here?'

'She didn't seem distressed,' put in Eunice timidly. 'Wouldn't you think if she was going to take poison she would have . . .'

'As a matter of fact,' Lylah Willis interrupted, 'Moya did hint to me before the meeting that she was upset about something.'

Mother Paul's bright gaze rested on Lady Willis. 'What did Moya hint?'

'She spoke to me for a moment when I arrived this afternoon. She said she felt I was in for a shock and she considered herself partly to blame if there was any disgrace. You heard her, Eunice.'

'Oh, Lylah,' the other wept, 'she was trying to tell you about Rianne coming to the reunion. I asked her to drop you a hint. You wouldn't have minded it so much coming from Moya. I . . . I knew you'd have been angry with me though.'

'Rianne!' exclaimed Lady Willis with an almost insane fury, her fleshy jaw quivering. 'That woman brings nothing but trouble. She's at the bottom of this. She's—'

'That's enough, Lylah!' said Janet authoritatively. 'Pull yourself together. And just remember Mother Paul is here.'

'Oh, dear, I wish you wouldn't,' murmured the nun. 'So enlightening!'

The curtains behind them moved and the inspector emerged. Mother Paul introduced him to the committee members individually. He surveyed them for a moment and then said quietly: 'I am sorry to have kept you, ladies! Is everyone here now?'

'All but Sue—Miss Berry. I sent her to find the two small girls who were waiting at table. Here they come now!' Lady Willis pulled her furs about her and tilted her head arrogantly. 'I am Lady Willis, Inspector. I presume you have heard of my husband, Sir Hammond Willis?'

Savage drew out a notebook and pressed the top of a ball point pen. 'And your address please, Lady Willis?'

'My husband knows your Commissioner quite well. I'm sure you would not like him to hear of any adverse reports concerning your treatment of Sir Hammond's family.'

'Indeed, no,' agreed Savage politely. 'If you would just give me your address, please, then I will be able to ask the other ladies for theirs.'

'It's quite absurd,' muttered Lylah petulantly after Savage had written it down and moved on. 'I'll see that the Commissioner hears of our being lined up like a bunch of criminals.'

'You needn't bother complaining on my account, Lylah,' said Carol crisply. 'If Ham hears what a nuisance you're making of yourself, he'll be more likely to apologise than complain.'

'I know how Lylah feels,' said Eunice. 'It's all so sordid.'

The inspector silenced her. 'Now I understand you ladies were sitting at the same table as the deceased, Miss Curran, and that afternoon tea had been served. Did any of you see anything that might throw light on what happened? Did anyone, for example, see Miss Curran eat or drink anything other than what you all had?'

'Of course we didn't,' snapped Lylah. 'We were all too occupied having to listen to Rianne May.'

'Rianne May?' Savage showed mild surprise. 'The television star?'

'She's not here just now,' explained Sue lamely. 'She left just after . . . after we noticed Miss Curran was ill. But if you want to talk to her, I'm sure she'll be at home. She and I share a flat. I'm her secretary.'

'She ran away,' sneered Lylah.

'A normal psychological reaction,' Janet said briskly. 'Some people are paralysed on receiving a tremendous shock, some run round in circles as it were, others just run.' She looked her companions over clinically. 'You all followed one pattern or another.'

'What did you do, Doctor?' asked Savage, almost casually.

'My reactions are more disciplined than most people's. They have to be: I'm a doctor. When I saw Moya in distress I naturally tried to do what I could for her.'

'I understand it was you who told everyone she had been poisoned. Is that right?'

Janet reddened. 'Maybe I shouldn't have blurted it out quite like that, but cyanide is pretty unmistakable and it was all so sudden and unexpected — the last thing one would expect at a reunion meeting. Even doctors are human, you know.'

Dear Janet was so brave,' spoke up Eunice, who never could pass an opportunity to come to another's assistance. 'She even tried mouth to mouth resuscitation.'

Savage's brows went up again. 'And you had already diagnosed cyanide poisoning? Didn't you realise the danger of that?'

Janet shrugged. 'I reacted as any doctor would. It is my business to try to save life. My only mistake was to tell everyone my diagnosis. Naturally there was a terrific hullabaloo. Then I looked to see what she had been eating and drinking. I couldn't detect any odour in her cup — which made me think later that she might have taken the poison herself directly.'

'Of course she took it herself,' declared Lylah, with finality.

'I'm sorry, Lady Willis, but we have found a tea-cup which might have contained the poison. There are certain indications.'

If it was in her tea then someone must have put it there,' said Janet, completely surprised by the inspector's statement. 'Who?'

'Yes, who?' agreed Savage suavely, and looked down at his notebook.

'I might be able to help you,' said Sue quietly. 'No, please, I'm not trying to cause a sensation. It was Moya, but she didn't know what she was doing. You see, there was no sugar on the table and — '

'Rianne's saccharine!' exclaimed Carol. 'How stupid can we be not to have hit on it at once!'

'I knew that woman was at the bottom of this!' said Lylah

triumphantly.

'But surely Rianne wouldn't want to harm Moya?' Eunice said. 'She didn't even know her before today.'

'The poison was not meant for Moya,' Carol put in as if ruminating to herself. 'It was for Rianne. She said so herself before she ran off.'

Sue addressed the inspector: 'There was an anonymous letter a few days ago saying she was going to die soon. It was amongst the fan mail the studio sent up to our flat—'

'Where is this letter, Miss Berry?'

'I . . . I'm afraid I destroyed it. Rianne told me to. She didn't want to tell the police—she said it was a hoax—but I think she was frightened, all the same.'

'With very good reason it seems,' commented Savage dryly. 'What about this saccharine of Miss May's?'

'She always carried a little bottle of tablets in her bag. She shook some on to the cloth at afternoon tea and we all took one—that is, those who wanted to sweeten their tea.'

'So you see, Inspector, it is as I maintained from the start. This dreadful business has nothing to do with any of us,' said Lylah Willis.

The inspector eyed her thoughtfully for a moment and then spoke to Mother Paul: 'If Miss Berry wouldn't mind staying behind, the other ladies may leave now.'

'You mean we're to go?' asked Eunice, blinking. 'I don't quite follow . . .'

'Oh, Mummy, can't you see?' exclaimed Jillian, who was an avid reader of detective stories. 'One of Miss May's saccharine tablets contained the poison. It was put in ages and ages ago. Anyone might have been poisoned.'

'Jilly, what are you saying?'

'The child's right, Eunice. Any one of us might have taken that particular tablet,' Janet Gordon declared.

'Oh, Janet, how horrible! Poor, poor Moya!'

'Just thank your lucky stars you're alive to do the weeping,' Janet returned grimly. 'Rianne can thank hers, too.'

'I feel sick,' Carol said. 'Like the time I nearly got skittled by a car.'

'I take it we won't be worried further by your attentions, Inspector,' said Lady Willis coldly, as she gathered up her handbag. 'Goodbye, Mother Paul. I'll be in touch with you about convening an M.P.S.A. meeting at some later date. There was quite a lot of business we were prevented from tackling, thanks to my colleagues' enthusiasm for Rianne May. Sue, would you come and see me tomorrow morning? I think you should be able to take over Moya's position on the executive.'

'Really, Lylah, you're the limit!' exploded Janet. 'Someone has been killed and all you can think of is your blasted committee. Let me get out of here before I really lose my temper.'

After they had gone, the inspector turned to the nun. 'What Miss Berry has just said does seem to throw a different light on the case.'

'Perhaps nothing to do with Maryhill after all,' she agreed. 'Poor little Moya! Such a wicked, wanton murder!'

One of his squad approached Savage. 'We've finished now, Inspector. Shall I tell the ambulance men to come in?'

Savage nodded at them and then turned to Mother Paul again. 'Is there somewhere I could have a little talk to Miss Berry?'

'One of the parlours,' she suggested, indicating to them to follow her. Out of the hall, she shepherded them along the dim corridors and presently threw open a door. 'You won't be disturbed here.'

'Please stay, won't you?' Savage invited her as she seemed to withdraw, albeit reluctantly. 'Mother Paul has solved my cases for me before,' he added with a twinkle to Sue. The girl laughed a trifle nervously, then she recalled some vague gossip relating to the time when Mother Paul had been Warden at a women's college.

'Nothing of the kind,' said the nun, seating herself in a billow of serge skirts. 'On that occasion I happened to be closer to the scene than Mr Savage, Sue, that's all. You can see little odd things that an outsider must necessarily miss.'

The inspector's eyes lost their gleam of humour, but the tone of his voice remained quiet and genial. 'If Rianne May was the intended victim, Miss Berry, then you are the one closest to the scene this time.'

She looked at him fearfully and then at Mother Paul, who gave her an encouraging smile.

'All I want is your co-operation,' the inspector reassured Sue.

'Tell me how you came to be her secretary first.'

'I owe her a great deal,' Sue began and went on to explain her meeting with Rianne in London and its aftermath.

'This letter,' Savage said, 'to your knowledge, was it the only one she received?'

Sue nodded.

'And how did she react to it?'

'She was shocked, I could tell. Afterwards she declared it was a hoax, but I got the impression that she knew what was behind it. I don't mean that she expected it or could guess who sent it, but that she associated it with something—or someone. She showed the same sort of fear then as she did this afternoon.'

'She has never spoken to you of any secret worry?'

'Never! In fact, I have never seen Rianne behave like that before.'

'It's a pity you destroyed that letter. Could you describe what it looked like as precisely as possible, please?'

From the letter, he led her into giving her account of the events surrounding Moya Curran's death. His questions were both patient and skilful as he cross-checked each bit of information that Sue was able to give, while all the time Mother Paul listened with avid attention.

'Can you tell me, Miss Berry, of anyone connected with Rianne May who might harbour a grudge against her? A grudge that would be capable of producing murder?'

Sue shook her head. 'She has been here for such a short time. I've no doubt that everyone at the studio had probably heard of her before her arrival, but only Sir Hammond Willis had actually met her. He was in London on a business trip and asked her to come out on a contract. No one else—' she stopped short, frowning slightly.

'Yes, Miss Berry?' prompted the inspector.

'The floor manager for Rianne's show. He knew her in British television, so he said. His name is Eric Watts.'

Savage made a note of the name. 'Who else is connected with Miss May's show?'

Sue gave names reluctantly. 'But they wouldn't want to harm Rianne or even send her a threatening letter. Their jobs and reputations depend on her welfare. A successful show means a great deal to the careers of a lot of other people besides its star—the scriptwriter and the camera crew and the . . . the director.'

'You're making my job hard, Miss Berry,' observed Savage with a touch of irony. 'Now, this bottle of saccharine tablets! Could anyone have interfered with it at the tea table today?'

'No, I'm sure no one could,' Sue replied in a small voice. 'Rianne took the bottle straight from her bag and shook some of the tablets on to the cloth. We all took one, except Lady Willis and another committee woman, who don't take sugar.'

'The other ladies at the table—they all knew Miss May?'

'All but Moya. But it's years since they've seen her. And they were only schoolgirls then.'

'How did they behave towards her?'

'Everyone seemed genuinely thrilled to see her.'

'Everyone?' asked Savage. 'I had an impression of hostility on the part of Lady Willis.'

Sue hesitated, glancing uncertainly at the nun. 'I think Lylah is a bit jealous at the fuss being made over Rianne.'

Savage looked at her with a question in his eyes. 'Yes, that was the impression I got—jealousy,' he agreed smoothly and Sue was grateful for his tact.

But Mother Paul rather confounded them by saying with devastating simplicity: 'Poor foolish Lylah with all her committees and charities. Her home life can't be happy. Such a difficult child Sandra is, too!'

Savage's mouth twitched appreciatively. Then he asked Sue what Rianne's attitude had been at seeing her old schoolfriends again.

Sue smiled ruefully. 'She was thoroughly enjoying herself, that is until the . . . the murder. She wasn't very popular at school, you see, and to come back to Maryhill a famous personality was a triumph. This time she did the patronising and the snubbing.'

'She couldn't have made herself any more popular then,' observed Savage dryly. 'However, we can hardly account for anyone wanting to murder her for her unpopularity. I think I'll go along and see the lady now. Perhaps you could direct me. Miss Berry?'

'I'll be glad of the lift,' said Sue, rising.

The inspector turned to Mother Paul and addressed her in a quietly sympathetic voice: 'The dead girl, Mother Paul, has she any family? They should be warned, I feel, before my men are through with the autopsy. A policeman is always an unexpected shock, you know . . .'

'One of the Sisters has gone there,' Mother Paul assured him. 'Such a dreadful business, Inspector.'

She escorted them to the front door, her hand resting lightly on Sue's arm. 'You'll keep in touch with me, won't you, dear child? Such an anxious time—poor Rianne! Success never ensures happiness. Dear me, is that your car, Inspector? So splendid . . .'

'It belongs to the studio,' Sue explained in surprise as she recognised the studio car. 'Rianne must have sent Ted back to pick me up.'

Ted got out of the Mercedes in answer to her beckoning finger. 'Is Rianne all right?' Sue asked sharply. 'Did you take her home?'

'She's all right. Sir Hammond is with her.' He eyed the nun and the inspector cautiously. 'What's been happening?'

'Didn't Rianne tell you? One of the women was poisoned during the afternoon tea. We feel she might have been murdered in mistake for Rianne.'

His face did not change its calm expression and Sue felt oddly irritated with him. It was as if murder to Ted was an everyday happening. 'She just came tearing out,' he explained. 'You know the way she always dashes, and told me to take her straight back to the flat and then to get hold of Sir Hammond immediately.'

'Well, so long as she's safe. Mother Paul, Inspector, this is Ted Brown. He was appointed Rianne's bodyguard. He's one of the security officers.'

The nun looked up at him. 'Goodness, you're even taller than Inspector Savage! So easy to see you're both policemen.'

Ted grinned down at her as Savage explained with some curtness the difference between the Victoria Police and security officers hired by big business.

'I'm going with Inspector Savage, Ted,' Sue explained. 'He wants to interview Rianne. You can follow us. Goodbye, Mother Paul, I'll come and see you soon, I promise.'

The nun embraced her fondly and stood at the top of the steps until the two cars drove off. Then, with a little sigh, she turned as though to go inside, but suddenly changed her mind and descended the steps instead. It had been a trying afternoon: a short walk round the garden would be soothing.

And there were one or two odd little matters she wanted to think about . . .

4

The sound of Sue letting the inspector and Ted into the flat brought Sir Hammond Willis out of the living-room. He was a handsome, heavily built man, as commanding in appearance as his wife. But whereas Lylah's self-assurance showed itself in arrogant and discontented lines, Sir Hammond's was contained behind a bland and affable veneer. He was rumoured to be a man of as much power as wealth, with an anonymous finger in many other moneymaking pies besides his television company.

'I thought it was Rianne,' he remarked, and drained the whisky and soda he was carrying.

'Is Miss May not here?' demanded Savage sharply.

Sir Hammond eyed him with supercilious calm. 'She's just gone out for a moment. Is this a friend of yours, Miss Berry? Or yours, Brown?'

'Inspector Savage from Russell Street, C.I.B.,' introduced Sue nervously. Sir Hammond's manner always intimidated her.

Sir Hammond gave a slight shrug. 'Well, come on in. Can I offer you a drink, Inspector? I'm presuming you're not on duty.'

'Thank you, sir, but as it happens I am.'

Sir Hammond handed his glass to Ted but continued to survey the detective. 'My usual, please, Brown. Detective-Inspector, Criminal Investigation? Is something wrong then? Has anything happened to Rianne, Miss Berry?'

Savage answered for her: 'I came here to see Miss May in an official capacity. This afternoon she attended a gathering of past students at Maryhill College. During afternoon tea one of the women she was sitting with was poisoned. Miss May left before we had time to question her regarding the incident.'

Ted carefully and opportunely put the replenished glass back into Sir Hammond's outstretched hand. 'Good heavens!' the big man spluttered. 'What an appalling thing! I was wondering why Rianne sent for me so urgently. But you're surely not thinking she had anything to do with this woman's death—I take it she is dead, else you wouldn't be here?'

Savage nodded grimly. 'Cyanide.'

Sir Hammond's hand twitched, spilling some of the liquid. 'Suicide? No, surely not—not at a public gathering. Murder, Inspector?'

'We're inclined to the theory that it was an accidental murder,' replied Savage enigmatically.

Sir Hammond gave him an impatient look. 'Just what does that mean?'

'It is under consideration that the poison was meant, not for the dead woman, but for Miss May.'

'For Rianne? But that's incredible! Who would want to murder Rianne? Are you thinking she might be able to tell you, Inspector?'

I'm hopeful at least that she might be able to give us some leads,' replied Savage cautiously.

Sir Hammond seemed almost to be talking to himself as he walked up and down the room. 'Someone planned to kill Rianne at that afternoon tea—a cold-blooded, premeditated murder?' He turned abruptly. 'I suppose you have your suspicions already, Inspector?'

'At the moment the field of suspects is a pretty large one. Until I interview Miss May and hear what she can suggest, the poison could have been administered by anyone.'

'I don't follow you, Inspector.'

'We're inclined to think the poison was administered by means of a tablet planted among the saccharine tablets Miss May uses in place of sugar. She brought a bottle of tablets out, during the afternoon tea and most of the women took one. Unknowingly, a Miss Moya Curran chose the one that had been poisoned.'

'Shocking! Shocking!' repeated Sir Hammond. He continued pacing the room, obviously shaken.

Presently Savage asked: 'Why did Miss May send for you so urgently if not to tell you what had happened?'

'I don't know. I haven't seen her yet.'

'Haven't seen her!' exclaimed Savage sharply. 'Then where is she?'

Sir Hammond paused and looked at him. 'She went out—down to the local for some gin, I think she said. She should be back at any moment. Miss Berry, have a look in that waste-paper basket, will you? I threw the note she left for me in there.'

Savage got there first. He unfolded a crumpled piece of paper. Sue read Rianne's familiar scrawl over his arm. 'Dying for a Martini—no gin anywhere. Will get some at Clauscen's. Plenty of whisky though, so tell Ted to mix you a drink and please wait. Won't be long. R.'

Savage raised his eyes. 'Then Miss May wasn't here when you arrived. How did you get in then?'

'I have a key,' replied Sir Hammond smoothly. 'This flat is the property of my company, you know.'

Savage turned to Ted Brown. 'I thought you said you left Miss May with Sir Hammond.'

'I thought I did, too. When we got back here she got on the phone to Sir Hammond and—'

'I was at my golf club, Inspector,' Sir Hammond interposed. 'Rianne sent Brown to fetch me. He dropped me at the door of the flat and asked if he could go back to Maryhill to pick up Miss Berry. By the way, was my wife there this afternoon?' he asked casually.

'Yes, she was there, Sir Hammond.'

Sir Hammond examined the fingernails of each hand. 'I suppose she was sitting with Rianne? And young Carol?'

'We were all at the same table,' answered Sue.

'Where is Clauscen's?' asked Savage.

'Just a block or so down the street. They know Rianne there.'

Savage went to the window and looked down in silence for several moments. 'No sign of her,' he said finally. 'May I use the phone, Miss Berry?' He thumbed through the directory rapidly.

'She's probably got caught up with someone she knew,' suggested Sue uneasily.

Savage dialled a number without replying, and then handed the receiver to her. 'You enquire if Miss May is there, Miss Berry. We don't want to arouse too much interest.'

'Quite right!' approved Sir Hammond. 'I appreciate your discretion, Inspector.'

'They're paging her,' reported Sue presently, and her voice was even more uneasy. The desk clerk had stated definitely that he had not seen Miss May come in, neither had the licensee.

'Well, Miss Berry?' asked Savage, when the girl slowly replaced the receiver.

'She's not there. No one remembers having seen her today.'

Savage was silent. He looked out into the street again.

'What now?' asked Sir Hammond sharply. 'Do you think she may have been kidnapped, Inspector?'

'Perhaps,' replied Savage briefly. 'Or else gone into hiding.'

'Why should Rianne want to do that?'

'Fear!'

'Fear? What on earth has Rianne to be afraid of? Now come, Inspector, I think you're being a little hasty. Rianne is a remarkable woman, not like other women in the least. She's probably gone off for a while without thinking. I'm sure she'll be back soon.'

Savage looked at him. 'Yet only a moment ago you yourself brought forward the kidnapping idea, Sir Hammond.'

'Perhaps I was being a little hasty, too,' admitted Sir Hammond.

'No,' said Savage. 'It's a definite possibility. Look down into the street! Late Sunday afternoon, not a soul about. Someone could have enticed her into a car without causing a disturbance.'

'But why? For what reason—money?'

Savage shook his head grimly. 'You seem to have forgotten, Sir Hammond, that one attempt has already been made on Miss May's life.'

'Then what are you waiting for?' demanded the other. 'Get going, man, if you think Rianne is in any danger.'

Savage said coldly: 'Not so fast! There are three possibilities to consider. First, Miss May may yet appear—your own suggestion again, Sir Hammond. Secondly, she may have gone into hiding either for fear of her life or because she does not want to face police questioning—or both! Then again, she may have been kidnapped.'

'Which possibility do you favour?' asked Sir Hammond impatiently.

'I have not yet met Miss May, but I think she might be a frightened and foolish woman. She may still be running from what took place this afternoon without thinking, believing that she was intended to be the victim. I am going to give her a few hours during which time I must call on Moya Curran's parents. If she doesn't appear of her own accord, then we will start looking for her.'

'But what if she has been kidnapped?' cried Sue, jerked out of the daze she had fallen into after telephoning Clauscen's Hotel.

Savage turned to her and she flinched at the expression on his face. 'If that is the case, Miss Berry, then the chances are that she is already dead.'

'How can you be so sure?' asked Sir Hammond angrily.

'Because it looks as if someone has already tried to carry out the threat made against her. And if that is so, the only reason for abduction would be to murder Miss May. A ruthless killer is not likely to procrastinate at this stage.'

'But you think she will come back, don't you?' said Sue, her voice trembling.

'I can only say I hope so. Miss Berry,' Savage replied, his voice kinder.

'What's all this talk about a threat?' demanded Sir Hammond. 'I knew nothing of any threat.'

Sue answered him: 'A few days ago there was an anonymous letter in the studio mail. Rianne tried to make light of it, but I could see she was very upset.'

'Why wasn't I informed? Did you know of this, Brown? Your job is to look after Miss May.'

'He knows nothing about it. Rianne forbade me to tell anyone,' Sue put in quickly. 'She told me to destroy the letter.'

Savage turned to Ted, whose expression was as impassive as ever. 'Has anything happened to make you uneasy about Miss May's welfare since you have been looking after her? Take your time and think.'

'I can't think of anything,' Ted said. 'Most times I'm just driving her from one place to another, or hanging around the studio. She has asked me to take messages to people—'

'Which people?' the inspector asked.

'Sir Hammond and others.'

'What others?' asked Savage, after a brief glance at Sir Hammond.

'Well, there's Mr Petrie, the director of her show. Twice she sent me to break some appointment she had with him. Then there were the cuff-links I had to pick up for the camera man, Greg Oliphant. Miss May was always giving little gifts to people. I once saw her putting money into an envelope which she told me to give to Mr Watts.'

'The floor manager? What did he say when you gave it to him?'

'Nothing. Just put it in his pocket without opening it.'

'Do you know if Miss May has given money to Watts on other occasions?'

Ted's brow wrinkled. 'Not to Mr Watts, but she gave Mr Bexhill a tenner once. Told him to take his girl out.'

'Johnny Bexhill, the script writer for Rianne's show,' explained Sue quietly to Savage's glance of enquiry. 'He's engaged to Carol Frazer, one of the girls at Maryhill this afternoon.'

'A decent young fellow, Inspector,' said Sir Hammond genially. 'But I'm afraid my young sister-in-law has expensive tastes. I doubt if the engagement will last.'

The telephone rang suddenly, and even Savage seemed to start towards it. Then he said: 'You answer it, Miss Berry. And if it's Miss May, don't let her go.'

Sue took up the receiver. 'Hello?'

'Sue? This is Eunice Hurley. Is Hammond there? Poor Lylah is in such a state.'

'Yes, he's here,' said Sue. 'Does Lylah want to speak to him, Eunice?'

'No, no, Sue! She doesn't know I'm trying to locate him. She just guessed he'd be with that woman . . . Oh, dear, I didn't mean that, but Lylah keeps calling her . . . How is Rianne, Sue?'

'Rianne?' repeated Sue, her eyes on Savage, who was making a signal to her. 'Oh, Rianne's all right, thank you, Eunice,' she added.

'He should be at home with his wife, Sue.'

'Yes, I suppose so,' Sue said, uncomfortably aware that Sir Hammond must guess what was being said.

'Try and get him to come home, Sue. Poor Lylah, she's—'

'I'll do my best, Eunice.' Sue put the receiver back slowly, wondering how she could explain Eunice's plea, and found Sir Hammond looking at her with kindly eyes.

'My wife's sycophantic friend! What a pity *she* did not pick up the cyanide tablet. More things are wrought by meddling friends than this world dreams of. If you have finished with me, Inspector, I must go. I gather you don't want anything said about Rianne's disappearance for the moment?'

'Not for a few hours, if you please, Sir Hammond. The dead girl's parents may throw a different light on the matter; although I doubt it.'

'You will let me know what moves are being made for Rianne's recovery?'

'I'll come and see you tomorrow. There are a few people at your television station I'd like to interview.'

'Yes, I was afraid you might.' Sir Hammond nodded briefly to Sue and asked Ted to find him a taxi.

Alone with Sue, Savage said: 'I know this is a distasteful question, Miss Berry, but is Miss May having an affair with Sir Hammond?'

'Not in actual fact, to my knowledge,' the girl replied. 'But things have gone far enough for Lady Willis to have grounds for jealousy.'

'Far enough to constitute a motive for murder?'

Sue looked at him aghast, unable to speak.

Savage said with a nod: 'Yes, I've seen that look before, Miss Berry. It appears when a person realises suddenly that a murderer is not a vague, remote figure but someone real and well-known, perhaps even a friend.'

'Lylah is not a friend,' stammered Sue. 'I don't care for her much, but she wouldn't . . . she couldn't—'

'Couldn't she?' There was a note of cynicism in Savage's query. 'Then what about her friend who is always making matters worse by trying to make them better?'

'Eunice? You mean, would Eunice try to kill Rianne for Lylah's sake?' Sue thought for a moment, then she replied frankly: 'Eunice is a toady and the sort of woman who thrives on petty intrigue. She would only do as much for Lylah as she would get back.' After a moment's hesitation, she added: 'Rianne has by no means been the first woman to be connected with Sir Hammond.'

'Yes, I think we'll have to find some less obvious motive,' agreed Savage. 'What about Dr Gordon and Miss Frazer?'

Sue looked at him with troubled eyes. 'I was under the impression that you felt the murderer was far removed from the Maryhill set. I could swear that no one had access to Rianne's saccharine bottle at the table.'

'Just routine questions, Miss Berry,' he said reassuringly. 'Are you quite sure Dr Gordon and Rianne hadn't met since their schooldays?'

'From the gist of their conversation I'd say they hadn't seen each other for years. Carol, of course, is in charge of the studio make-up room, so she knows Rianne fairly well.'

'Let's consider the studio, er, set,' he suggested. 'Would anyone amongst them have had an opportunity to doctor Rianne's saccharine?'

'Well, Rianne was always leaving her bag lying about and sending someone to find it. The saccharine she uses is a patent brand. I suppose the bottle itself could have been exchanged without her noticing it.'

'Who knew of her habit of using saccharine instead of sugar?'

Sue gave a weary smile. 'Anyone who had watched her drinking tea or coffee—which she even does in a commercial on her show.'

Savage went to the window again and looked down. 'What was Miss May wearing today?' he asked casually.

'A dark blue frock—Dior, I think. Anyway, she bought it in Paris. She also had a mink stole and a hat to match.'

'Not the sort of thing she'd wear to run down to the corner for a bottle of gin,' Savage decided. 'Do you think she might have changed when she came in?'

'I'll go and check if you like,' offered Sue.

'Yes, do that—oh, and Miss Berry! If you should see Brown, tell him to come in again.'

'He's probably stayed downstairs. He has a room near the garage. You can ring through to him. The number is just by the phone on a list there.'

In Rianne's bedroom there was no sign of disorder except for a pile of discarded clothes on the elaborate chaise-longue and one of the cupboard doors standing ajar, showing that Savage's guess about her having changed was right. Sue opened the mirrored doors wide and went through the racks of clothes, finally deciding that Rianne must be wearing her check slacks and a pullover and the suede car coat that bore the Fifth Avenue label.

She went back to the living-room to report. Savage was still on the phone, his back to the door. She heard him say: 'Very well, Brown. But you must realise I'll have to check on your story.' Then he cut off the call and began dialling another number. 'I won't be a moment, Miss Berry. The people at the morgue might have some information.'

Sue could not repress a slight shiver as she listened to his terse questions. Finally Savage said: 'Yes, we've been working on the assumption that it was cyanide. My men are already checking all possible channels. You'll let me have the confirming report as soon as possible?'

He replaced the receiver and turned to look at Sue—a speculative, measuring glance with a touch of humour in it which rather puzzled her. She was beginning to understand why Mother Paul thought so highly of him. He was a man who did not waste time with unnecessary questions.

'Rianne did change, but the rest of her things are there.' She gave him precise details which he noted down. 'Her make-up case and overnight bag are there, too,' she added.

'That doesn't look so good,' he remarked, closing his book with a snap. 'It looks as if she did intend just to go to Clauscen's. I'll leave you this number, Miss Berry, should Miss May happen to return. If I don't hear from you by midnight, we'll start a more exhaustive search than is being conducted right now. Which means, of course, that the news of her disappearance will have to be made public.'

Sue accompanied him to the door of the flat. One foot over the threshold he turned back to ask: 'By the way, Miss Berry, suppose you had planned to poison someone, how would you go about obtaining cyanide?'

'I wouldn't . . . I wouldn't have a clue,' she stammered.

'Neither have I—yet,' replied Savage cheerfully.

Rianne did not return, and early the next morning Sue began to realise what Savage had implied when he said her disappearance would have to be made public. She jumped nervously out of bed when the telephone rang after a night spent listening for it or for Rianne's key turning in the door.

'Suzanne?' asked a lilting, alert voice.

'Yes, who is it?' She mumbled wearily, shivering in the cold living-room. She hadn't stopped to put a dressing-gown over her thin pyjamas.

'Dominus vobiscum, dear child! Did I get you out of bed?'

'Oh, Mother Paul.' Because she was tired and cold and frightened, Sue burst into tears, as a child weeps in the safe arms of its mother after a nightmare. 'Mother Paul, Rianne has gone—disappeared! The police don't know whether she has been kidnapped or . . . or just run away. She wasn't here yesterday when we—'

'Hush, Sue, don't cry! Dear me, so difficult to comfort anyone over a telephone!'

Sue gulped. 'I'm sorry. I'm all right now. Why are you ringing? It's awfully early, isn't it? I don't suppose . . . You haven't heard anything about Rianne, have you, Mother Paul?'

The nun's voice sounded apologetic as she said: 'I forgot the outside world's day doesn't start at the same time as ours. Such a delightful part of the day, too! The garden looks so fresh. But those dreadful headlines lying in the middle of the lawn!'

Sue caught a mental picture of the nun breathing in the keen morning air on a prayer which stopped short at the sight of the newspaper lying on the wet grass, where the paper boy had flung it over the convent wall.

'What did they say, Mother Paul?'

'Mostly about Rianne. A photograph of Lylah, too, in some sort of uniform—Red Cross, I think. Poor Moya—outshone even in death! The police state that they have reason to think there is a connection between the murder and the disappearance of the famous television star. A nation-wide hunt is being conducted and anyone knowing the whereabouts, etc., etc. Sue, dear, what happened after you left Maryhill yesterday?'

Sue told her, omitting no detail. It was a relief to unburden herself. Now and then, when she paused for breath, she could hear the sound of bells being gently rung or a rush of soft feet and swinging rosary beads passing the telephone. They were strangely comforting noises, as was the nun's serene voice when she asked: 'And what is to happen now?'

'Inspector Savage is going to the studio this morning to interview everyone there.'

'Then you'll be seeing him? I don't wish to harass the dear man—such a confusing case—but there are one or two points I would like to discuss with him. Will you tell him, Sue, and ask him to call here?'

Rather dubiously, the girl promised. Without Rianne, she did not know exactly what her working day was to be. But Ted Brown solved the problem when he knocked later at the door of the kitchen where Sue was forcing herself to eat a late breakfast as she read the newspapers.

He was dressed in his uniform and gave her an anxious look. 'Sir Hammond phoned through. He wants you in his office. The police are with him.'

'Any news about Rianne?'

'Not a word. You don't look as if you slept much.'

'I didn't, but you needn't rub it in. I know I look a fright,' replied Sue irritably. She went away to collect letters and papers, stuffing them into a briefcase. When at the studio she used a corner of Rianne's dressing-room in which to do her work.

Presently, sitting beside him in the Mercedes, she said with an effort: 'Ted, I'm sorry I snapped at you. I'm tired and worried and everything's like a ghastly nightmare.'

His expression of concern vanished and he pushed his cap to the back of his fair clump of hair. 'That's all right by me. Be as nasty to me as you like if it makes you feel any better.'

'It doesn't make me feel better when you're always so amiable. I'd much prefer you to snap back. Do you like people treading all over you? I don't think I've ever seen you upset.'

'I guess I'm not the snapping kind,' he replied. 'I'm the quiet type.'

'You can say that again,' muttered Sue callously. His eyes came round to her enquiringly, so she added hastily: 'Sometimes I think you only act that way just to be superior. What did Inspector Savage want you for?'

'You mean when he rang down yesterday? Were you there then?

He said you were going through Miss May's clothes.'

'I heard him say he was going to check on your story. What story? You haven't been doing anything foolish, have you?'

'Oh, he was just asking me about the job.'

'Well, I hope you answered him truthfully,' said Sue slowly. 'He's not a man to try to deceive and I wouldn't like you to get into any trouble. I think he trusts me, so if there is anything you haven't told him that he is likely to find out, you'd better tell me right away and I . . .'

'I think I can look after myself,' Ted said and there was something in the way he said it which made Sue flush with shame. But a second later he said amiably, his mouth twitching with laughter, 'I can't remember all my misdemeanours but I'll give it all serious thought later and let you know.'

'Yes, do that,' she said shortly, regretting her protective impulse and hating him for making her feel cheap.

He dropped her at the imposing entrance to the studio and drove off to park the car in the space allotted to it in the extensive grounds. Sue went into the building. She attracted many curious glances and several people stopped her to exclaim about the murder and Rianne's disappearance, She answered the questions briefly, not committing herself, and tried to ignore the glances.

Sir Hammond Willis's secretary greeted her with polite hostility. 'Sir Hammond has been waiting quite some time, Miss Berry.'

'I came as soon as I got his message,' replied Sue, and walked through to the Big Man's office.

'Here she is now!' Sir Hammond said brightly as she entered his softly carpeted, sound-proof office with its dove grey walls covered with enlarged photographs of various television personalities and stills of shows. He was as bland and affable as ever.

'Good morning, Miss Berry.' Inspector Savage nodded to her. 'No word, I imagine, from Miss May, else you'd have got into touch with me?'

'I was hoping you might have some news, Inspector. I wondered if Moya's parents . . . you were going to see them, you said.'

The inspector seemed to resent the question. 'It seems evident that there was no reason at all why Miss Curran should have been murdered—except accidentally. The important and urgent thing now is to try to find the whereabouts of Miss May. Sir Hammond suggested you might show me round the studios this morning.'

'I want Inspector Savage to be given the utmost cooperation,' Sir Hammond said genially. 'He is to go everywhere and see anyone he wants.'

'I'm particularly anxious to interview the other members of Miss May's show,' the inspector said curtly, addressing himself to Sir Hammond.

'They're rehearsing in Studio 2. Miss Berry will take you along there. We're going to run a special edition. One of our writers is working on the scheme now. Audiences are a curious phenomenon, Inspector. They'll be tuning in in their thousands tonight even though Rianne won't be appearing.'

'Then Miss May's disappearance is, in a way, publicity for the show?' There was no denying the scorn in the inspector's question.

Sir Hammond's smile lacked its usual warmth as he replied: 'Let us say we are attempting to turn a disadvantage into an advantage. We're hoping that, among the thousands watching, there will be someone who might be able to throw light on Rianne's whereabouts. I've instructed Bexhill to make this the pivot of the programme. Not only that, Inspector, but we are also offering a reward for information leading to her whereabouts.'

Sue, watching Savage, thought his habitual impassive expression showed annoyance. 'A large-scale hunt is under way, Sir Hammond. My office has already been inundated with possible leads. It seems Miss May has been seen everywhere from the Gold Coast to Alice Springs. What you propose is going to double the number of wild suggestions, and consequently our work.'

Sir Hammond looked at him haughtily. 'You object to the idea?'

'I consider it unnecessary,' replied Savage quietly.

'Good Heavens, man! You're a cool customer. A woman has disappeared, possibly been kidnapped and murdered, and you object to her friends trying to help.'

Savage's shoulders lifted almost imperceptibly. 'I appreciate your concern. Sir Hammond, but it would be much simpler if you could tell me where Miss May is hiding.'

Sir Hammond stared at him for a full moment. 'Be careful, Savage,' he said softly. 'I have no idea where Rianne is or what has happened to her.'

Savage returned his gaze steadily. He also paused before speaking: 'I'll try and sum up the situation as the police see it at the moment. Yesterday a woman was poisoned, apparently in mistake for Rianne May who had earlier received a threatening letter. We cannot question the intended victim because she has disappeared, but we do know that she is very frightened and therefore must have some idea of why her life could be in danger. If she was abducted to be got rid of, then where is her body? No trace of it has been found and the more time goes by without discovering her body, then the less likelihood there is that she has been murdered. The same applies to the kidnapping theory. Kidnappers go for ransom at once. The longer they hold a person, the more danger they are in of being uncovered. There has been no word from a kidnapper.'

'Are you quoting from the Manual of Criminal Investigations?' asked Sir Hammond Willis mockingly. 'Believe me, Inspector, I'll gladly go along with your idea that Rianne is alive and well.'

'I think she is most certainly alive,' said Savage. 'Alive but frightened in some way that precludes her asking for police protection, either by her own choice or because someone has coerced her. These are matters I have to find out, and they involve, not the thousands of unknown viewers of the *Rianne May Show*, but only those people with whom she has been in contact since her arrival in this country. And you can help me there—and Miss Berry.'

'You also consider that one of these people knows where she is?' observed Sir Hammond shrewdly.

'Miss May has been absent from Australia for many years. She is also a very well-known figure. Yes, I think to hide completely she needed someone's assistance—or someone's coercion.'

'I thought an accusation was the tenor of your remark a while back,' said Sir Hammond deliberately. 'I repeat—I don't know where Rianne May is.'

'You were the last person she was known to be in contact with, Sir Hammond. Did she ask you to hide her?'

'I won't attempt to remind you that I did not even see Rianne yesterday,' the other replied in a bored tone. 'No, Inspector, Rianne made no such request to me, nor am I, for some fantastic reason, holding her prisoner. Furthermore, as I do not subscribe to your summing up, I am even more resolved to put on her show the way I planned and to offer a reward.'

'I can't stop you, Sir Hammond.'

'I never allow anyone to stop me once I have made up my mind to anything, Inspector.'

For a moment there was silence, a strained and ominous silence. Then Sir Hammond broke the tension with one of his falsely genial laughs. 'Come, Inspector, I am giving you a free run of my television channel and a pretty guide to conduct you around. Isn't that enough co-operation? If it will relieve matters for your staff, I will put our own security on to taking enquiries and sifting the red herrings. Ted Brown can do the job. How's that?'

Savage looked at him keenly. 'That would be a help, Sir Hammond.'

Sir Hammond came round his desk and clapped him on the shoulder. 'Don't hesitate to call on me in any way. I want Rianne found and this shocking business cleared up as soon as possible. She's a very important property of mine.'

5

Studio 2 was an immense barnlike room as unglamorous as the wings of a theatre stage, the actual television sets taking up but a small area of the floor space. Sue, still not accustomed to being behind the scenes, always wondered how the melee of lights, cameras, props and personnel were ever sorted into a smooth and continuous programme.

A dance group was rehearsing when she and the inspector pushed through the heavy door with its green light indicating that filming was not in progress at the moment. People were talking and calling to each other and moving about, seemingly as restless and purposeless as insects. The musical director was scoring music frantically on the top of a piano which was being played by a young man with a cigarette drooping from his lower lip. The choreographer was shouting exhortations at his group and occasionally joining them in their prancing. The camera crews were taking angles while, under the direction of an audio technician, boom microphones were being raised and lowered to the danger of the unwary.

Sue, glancing at Inspector Savage, saw him regarding the scene with raised brows. 'So this is what goes on behind my television screen!' he said.

Sue laughed. 'Yes, I shall never cease to marvel at the way a wonderful show like Rianne's comes out of all the confusion. Though not really, I suppose. The director, Roger Petrie, does a marvellous job. It's all due to him.'

'Thank you, Sue,' said a quiet voice behind them. They swung round and if the inspector noticed the warm colour flooding Sue's face, he gave no sign of it.

Roger Petrie had come down from his booth in the gloomy upper regions under the studio roof. Like most personnel actively connected with television, he was quite young. He was also incredibly handsome in a dark, saturnine way and, even in his casual outfit of slim dark slacks and chunky pullover, looked as though his place should have been on the screen, not behind it.

'Roger Petrie, Inspector Savage,' Sue introduced them, trying to sound business-like and casual. But Roger Petrie continued to look at her in that serious, speculative, probing way as though trying to get to know her without all the preamble of acquaintance. She had the feeling that, one day soon, they would start off at a point most attracted couples don't reach for some time after the first meeting. It was a breath-taking, heart-warming thought, and Sue only half-listened as the two men went through the same preliminaries that had attended Rianne's name during the past twenty-four hours. She was wondering what there was about Roger Petrie that always made her feel alive, glowing. In his presence, she seemed to forget everything but the wonder of being near him. Even Rianne was temporarily forgotten—and Moya.

Suddenly ashamed, she pulled herself together.

'As Miss May's director,' said Savage, getting to his point, 'did you notice anything about her performance that might indicate she was either worried or frightened?'

'Not even the most demanding of directors could fault her work,' Roger Petrie said, after deliberating the question. 'She had occasional flashes of temper and irritability and that sort of thing, but no more than any other star I've directed.'

'Then you wouldn't say she had anything on her mind?'

'No, I don't think so.'

'I understand she broke a couple of personal appointments with you, each at the last moment. Wouldn't you say this betrayed a certain insecurity?'

Sue saw Roger glance at her briefly before he replied. 'Yes, I did ask Rianne out once or twice, but at the last minute something cropped up to prevent her coming.'

'Is that what she said?'

'More or less.'

'It was Miss May's bodyguard who told me of the broken dates. He said Miss May merely told him to tell you she couldn't keep the appointments.'

'I'm sorry if I misled you, Inspector,' said Roger steadily. 'I can't recall what Ted said exactly and was only assuming there was some sort of conventional excuse accompanying the message.'

'Did Miss May ever afterwards explain why she broke the dates in such arbitrary fashion?'

Roger smiled ruefully. 'No, never. In fact, she rather gave me the impression that she had forgotten I'd ever asked her.'

'In other words, her mind was occupied by something else. Which brings me back to my original question. Wouldn't you say that, by first accepting your invitations and at the last minute cancelling them by message and not referring to them again, she was not behaving normally?'

'You could be right,' agreed Roger politely.

Savage turned to Sue. 'What would you say, Miss Berry?'

'I didn't know Rianne had made any personal appointments with Roger.' Sue said it as if the whole idea were repugnant to her and the inspector looked hard at her.

'In a way they were duty dates,' said Roger swiftly. 'I usually try and offer our leads some off-camera hospitality.'

'Yes, of course,' replied Sue, clutching at the explanation. 'But I can't understand why Rianne didn't tell me. She usually did, un-less—' she stopped short. Roger was regarding her closely now and she looked away, an annoying flush mounting again in her cheeks.

Savage's tone was dry as he asked: 'Have you any idea at all, Mr Petrie, where Miss May is now?'

'No, none! I assure you, Inspector, we are all extremely anxious about her. We are hoping the special edition of her show will bring in some information.'

'Yes, Sir Hammond told me of the scheme,' replied Savage, even drier. 'I won't keep you any longer, but perhaps you won't object to my talking to a few of your staff—Mr Eric Watts, for example?'

'Oh, yes, sure! Go ahead. Eric!'

The floor manager peered round a camera and then advanced with obvious reluctance, pausing now and then to speak to someone so as to give the impression that he was not going to be hurried by anyone. He was a long, unhealthily thin man, slightly older than Roger Petrie, with an unhappy expression that was a token of the dyspepsia he was always trying to relieve by sucking peppermints. He gave Sue the barest nod and delivered some sour remarks about the progress of the rehearsal to Roger before he deigned to notice Savage. Then he said: 'I know you're from the police, but I don't see why you want to see me. I really haven't time to answer a lot of unnecessary questions.'

'Then I'll be as brief and to the point as possible,' returned Savage pleasantly.

Roger put a hand under Sue's elbow and drew her towards the stairs leading steeply to the director's booth. It was dim away from the lights, but she knew he was looking at her gravely and searchingly.

'It's awful about Rianne, isn't it?' she said foolishly. His habit of looking at her so intently before speaking was disconcerting.

'Tell me,' he said, still holding her arm. 'Why didn't Rianne tell you of her appointments with me? What was it you were going to say there with the inspector?'

'Nothing, really,' she protested, blushing furiously.

'But you looked so uncomfortable. I would like to know.' She felt annoyed at his persistence. 'I'm feeling even more uncomfortable now.'

'Are you? Then why? Please be frank with me, Sue.' His soft voice was intimately persuasive.

'Well, if you must know, I don't think Rianne mentioned your asking her out because she felt I might not like it. Though where she got the idea that I had any reason for objecting, I don't know. As you said just now, a director has certain obligations to a star.'

He seemed puzzled for a moment, then slid his hand down her arm to her hand. 'If I asked you to go out with me, would you break the date at the last moment?'

'That depends on where we were going,' she whispered, slightly at a loss.

'Is that what stopped Rianne?'

The question startled Sue. 'How do I know? I didn't even know—'

'No, no, of course,' he interrupted soothingly. 'Forgive me for being so tedious. Just let me say that I would very much like you to come out with me one evening—dinner and perhaps a show. Would you, Sue?'

'Yes, I'd like to,' she replied, suddenly shy. 'Thank you!'

'Fine!' He gave her another of his slow, grave looks, then added abruptly: 'That fellow Brown. What do you think of him?'

'Ted?' If Sue had not been so overwhelmed by the invitation she would have wondered at this question. Instead she smiled. 'Ted's all right. Conscientious, but not very communicative. Rather dull.'

'Yes, that's what I would have said too.' He nodded towards the inspector. 'Does he think someone here might have been responsible for that woman's death yesterday?'

'I don't know what he thinks,' replied Sue carefully. 'But anyone could have put the poison in Rianne's saccharine bottle, even quite some time ago.'

'It's a shocking business. No wonder you're looking strained.' He pressed her hand before releasing it. 'We'll make that date soon.' Turning, he ran lightly up the stairs.

Sue smiled foolishly to herself and glanced towards the inspector who was still with Eric Watts. 'I tell you I don't know anything about money,' she heard Eric say angrily. 'Either the clod was mistaken or else he is trying to discredit me for some reason. I flatly refuse to answer any more questions.'

'Sue!' She felt a touch on her arm and turned to find Johnnie Bexhill's anxious face confronting her.

'Oh, hello, Johnnie!' she said, reminded of Rianne's description of the show's script writer.

'Carol told me about yesterday, Sue. It's fantastic—unbelievable! Has anything been heard of Rianne yet?'

'No, nothing.'

He went on hurriedly, little beads of perspiration forming on his forehead in his agitation, 'Carol was terribly upset. She feels things more than other girls, you know. When I think she might have been the one to take that tablet!'

'Any one of us might have,' said Sue dryly.

'Who'd want to do such a thing to a lovely person like Rianne? She's so wonderful. That fellow with Eric—he surely doesn't suspect one of us. Why, what possible motive would there be?'

'I don't know, Johnnie,' said Sue wearily. 'The whole thing's a nightmare!'

'That's just what Carol said,' he agreed eagerly. 'Was I relieved that I'd waited for her! I tell you, Sue, I was pretty anxious last night when she wasn't at her flat when I called there. But it was all right, she'd just been to some doctor to get a sedative. That just shows how upset she was!'

'We were all rather shaken,' replied Sue absently. 'When did you hear about the murder, Johnnie?'

'I was here in my office all yesterday. I knew Carol was going to her school reunion. And Rianne. Some of the boys from the newsroom came to tell me it was going to be released on the night news spot. That must have been about seven-thirty. I was going to call on Carol, anyway, but when I heard how a friend of hers had been poisoned I just dropped everything and went there.'

'What did Carol say about Rianne?'

'That she was in a terrific flap because the poison was meant for her and that she'd rushed off before the police arrived and couldn't be found. I tell you, Sue, I felt like going out to look for Rianne myself when Carol said there was some talk of her having been kidnapped.'

'But Johnnie—' Sue broke off as Savage caught her eye warningly. He had let Eric go and had been standing within earshot a little behind Johnnie. 'Have you seen Carol since last night?' she asked carefully.

His face clouded. 'Only for a moment. I guess it's a natural reaction but she seems sort of quiet now, doesn't want to talk about it any more. She said she might see me in the canteen at lunch-time. Sue!'

'Yes, Johnnie?'

'I wish you'd drop into the make-up room and see how she is. She was so edgy with me, I can't help thinking she's got something on her mind.'

'I'll tell her you're expecting to have lunch with her,' promised Sue.

He looked anxious. 'You'll put it tactfully, Sue? Carol doesn't like to be ordered about, you know.'

'I'll be tactful,' promised Sue.

'Who was that?' asked Savage, when Johnnie had gone. Sue told him. And reported the gist of the conversation. 'He seems more concerned about his fiancée than where Rianne may be,' she ended.

'So Miss Frazer knew last night that Rianne had disappeared,' observed Savage pensively.

'Sir Hammond might have told her,' said Sue uncomfortably. 'I heard that he calls in to see her at her flat from time to time. She is Lylah's stepsister, you know.'

Savage made a sceptical sound but let it pass. 'Tell me. Miss Berry, which one amongst all these bright young men is Rianne's latest fancy?'

'Greg Oliphant?' asked Sue cautiously, not sure if the inspector was joking.

Savage's eyes twinkled. 'Mr Watts' description, not mine.'

'Just the sort of thing he would say,' remarked Sue with asperity. 'You'll find Greg on one of the cameras.'

'You don't care for Mr Watts?'

'No more than for any person who is so . . . so chronically disagreeable.'

'The chip on his shoulder is a fixture there. I wonder why?'

'He's supposed to have ulcers,' suggested Sue charitably. 'All floor managers get them.'

'He didn't like my questions. Did Miss May show any fear or even dislike of him?'

Sue frowned. 'Rianne didn't speak of him at all—which is strange, really, considering she knew him in England. According to Eric, he helped her along once.'

'Perhaps that might account for the gifts of money then—of which he disclaimed all knowledge, incidentally.'

Sue hesitated. 'Could Ted have made a mistake there, do you think?'

The inspector said wryly: 'He looks to you, then, like a fellow who makes mistakes—or tells lies?'

'No,' Sue stammered, confused. 'But . . .'

The inspector did not allow her to flounder on that matter. 'Do you handle Miss May's financial affairs, Miss Berry? Would you know if she has paid out any large sums of money?'

'I only look after the expenses the company allows her. Her salary is paid direct into her bank.'

'Then she could be blackmailed without anyone knowing?'

Sue wrinkled her forehead. 'But what would be the sense of a blackmailer trying to kill her?'

Savage nodded approval. 'Quite so. But it is possible that a blackmailer's possession of some secret Miss May is paying to keep hidden might also be the motive for a third person's wanting to silence her.'

'You mean if someone—say Eric—had been blackmailing Rianne, then what he knows about her is the key to the identity of the murderer?' She thought for a moment then added, rather shakily: 'What would happen to Eric then if. . .'

'It's an easy guess,' replied Savage grimly. 'However, it's not to say that Miss May was being blackmailed or that Eric Watts is blackmailing her. Where does Miss May bank?'

Sue told him. 'Would Eric have kidnapped Rianne?' she suggested hesitantly.

'To protect his investment, you mean? It is worth considering. So far our investigations regarding her possible whereabouts have led nowhere.'

'But why should Rianne be hiding?' exclaimed Sue despairingly. 'Why is she afraid, not only of the killer, but of the police?'

'Most probably she doesn't realise what a kind, understanding lot of blokes we are,' said Savage lightly. 'Let's see what Mr Greg Oliphant has to say, shall we?'

Greg, standing nonchalantly with one arm across his camera, watched them approach. He was little more than a boy, but there were lines on his attractively faun-like face that showed he was no innocent fledgling. 'Hi, Sue!' He looked up at the inspector jauntily. 'Eric tipped me off. I've neither murdered nor kidnapped Rianne, neither was I extorting.'

'Well, that has saved me a few questions,' replied Savage genially. 'There remains only two now—that is, assuming you are speaking the truth.'

Greg lowered his absurdly long lashes over his eyes. 'You'll have to take my truthfulness on trust. What are the other questions?'

'I understand that you and Miss May were on the way to becoming good friends.'

'Anything wrong with that?'

'Not if your feeling for Miss May is worthy of the name friendship. For instance, it would not be the act of a friend if you were hiding her from the police.'

'Oh? Why?' asked Greg, folding both arms over the camera and surveying Savage impishly.

'Because hiding is not the answer to Miss May's problems,' said Savage grimly. 'Her life has been threatened—she has already had one narrow escape. What is even more important, is the fact that an innocent girl has been murdered because of her. If she knows why and by whom her life is threatened, then she should do all in her power to help the police find the killer of the unfortunate woman whose life was taken instead.'

'Esprit de corps and all that!' remarked Greg meditatively. 'Personally it wouldn't worry me a damn who died instead of me as long as I was all right. I doubt if it would worry Rianne, either.'

'It would worry both of you if a charge of accessory after the fact was made,' said Savage sharply. 'Yes, it's quite possible, Mr Oliphant. So, for your own sake as much as for Miss May's, can you tell me where she is? Did she come to you for protection?'

'No, she did not!' answered Greg promptly.

'Have you any idea where she might be? Did she ever mention friends or places?'

Greg thought for a moment, then shook his head.

'One last question,' said Savage patiently. 'Did she ever tell you she was afraid of something or someone? Or did you, from her manner, ever suspect that she was?'

Greg unfolded his arms and straightened up. 'Yes, she was afraid,' he replied slowly. 'I don't know what about, though. As a matter of fact, I thought she was only being dramatic at the time. You don't believe everything a temperamental woman like Rianne says.'

'What did she say?'

'I'll try to remember. I took her for a drive one evening after a rehearsal. She said she wanted some fresh air so we drove round the coast awhile. Then we pulled up to look at the sea, and she started to ask some rather odd questions, as though she were fishing for something. I pretended to go along, though for the life of me I couldn't make out what she was driving at.'

'What were the odd questions?' asked Savage.

'It might sound silly, but I can't recall precisely.' Greg flushed and glanced at Sue. 'To be quite honest, I was a bit overwhelmed at being asked by a great star to take her out. I guess I was busy trying to make an impression.'

'I appreciate your candour, Mr Oliphant, but you must remember some part of what Miss May said, surely!'

'There was something about how wrong she'd been in thinking the Australian offer had come at the right time, and how lonely and frightening it was sometimes being famous, because people used you and sometimes you couldn't get out of their reach. Then she said it's easy to get caught in a web when you're young and ignorant and enthusiastic. I remember I tried to get her to explain that one but she said it was nothing to do with me after all. Then she laughed and . . . and ran her hands through my hair and asked me to kiss her. We drove home after that.'

'And you never tried to work out what she was getting at?'

'I thought no more about it. I had no intention of becoming deeply involved with Rianne. Quite frankly, I look after my own skin first, and the boss's girlfriend can be dangerous. I didn't want to be thrown out on my neck for upsetting the Big Man.'

'In other words, if Rianne had come to you asking for help you would have refused.'

'Quite likely,' Greg replied, jaunty once again. 'So you see, Inspector, I am completely detached from Rianne and her tortuous affairs.'

'Always assuming you can be trusted to tell the truth,' reminded Savage pleasantly. 'But until I find Miss May, everyone who knows her, from Sir Hammond down, is implicated in her affairs. I trust I make myself clear?' With that, he turned on his heel and made his way to the exit.

Sue gave Greg one withering look and followed. Outside in the corridor she asked Savage if he still wanted her as she should pick up Rianne's mail, which had probably been delivered to her dressing-room.

'You can do that presently,' he said in an absent tone. 'Did Rianne ever ask you vaguely probing questions, Miss Berry?'

'I don't think so. When I met her in London she wanted to know what I'd been doing and all that sort of thing. She listened sympathetically, but I wouldn't say she probed in any way.'

'Did you ever hear her at this . . . this "fishing" that camera boy spoke about?'

Sue thought for a moment. Then she said reluctantly: 'Well, the only thing I could term "fishing" in any way was Rianne wanting to know about Carol and her relationship with Sir Hammond. Rianne did get Carol talking about the row she had had with Lylah before Lylah turned her out. But there was probably nothing ulterior in her enquiries. People do tend to gossip while they're having their hair done or being made up. In fact, Carol herself said that . . .'

'What did Miss Frazer say?' asked Savage, as Sue hesitated.

She looked at him with troubled eyes. 'I'm sure it's not important, but yesterday before . . . before Moya died, when the girls were talking, a suggestion was made that everyone has something shameful in their lives that they would prefer to remain hidden. And Carol—I think because Rianne had snubbed her—said, if she wanted to, she would be able to find out a thing or two about Rianne, that the make-up room was always a good place for gossip.'

'What did Miss May say to this challenge?'

'It didn't seem to worry her in the least,' replied Sue lamely. 'She claimed that her life was an open book.'

Savage's brows went up. 'A strange remark in view of subsequent events. Perhaps Miss Frazer might be able to explain it. Where is the make-up department?'

'This way,' said Sue, not relishing her job as guide.

But Carol, far from showing any signs of uneasiness, greeted the detective's appearance pertly. 'I was hoping I wouldn't be left out. What's Sue been telling you about me? You don't mind if I go on working, do you?' She indicated an anonymous form draped in protective sheeting sitting in front of a long row of mirrors. 'Harry is due on camera in a quarter of an hour, and we've got to disguise the results of a night out. Wouldn't do for all his housewife fans to think he'd been a naughty lad, would it, Harry?'

The well-known face, the only part visible that is, scowled un-photogenically from the tilted head-rest of the make-up chair.

'I could wait until you had finished,' Savage suggested. Carol met his eye in the mirror. 'No, shoot! Don't worry about Harry. He's too busy working out how to make the housewives giggle. Besides I've got nothing to hide.'

'Like Miss May's, your life is an open book?'

Carol, who had been carefully shaping a stick of No. 5 with a tissue, glanced up again. This time she sought Sue's gaze. 'Sounds like the man's quoting. What gives?'

'Yesterday when Janet said everyone has something to hide and Rianne denied this, you hinted that you knew something she'd prefer to remain hidden,' explained Sue unhappily.

'I did?' countered Carol provokingly. 'I rather thought the point of that part of the conversation was Rianne having a crack at Janet.'

'Miss Frazer,' said Savage directly. 'Do you know where Miss May is, or can you suggest why she should have gone into hiding?'

'Hold still, Harry, I've nearly finished! Just a shadow to accentuate your cleft chin. The forties and over simply adore a dimpled chin—it's said to be the sign of a flirt. No, Inspector, I don't know where Rianne is.'

'And the second part of my question, Miss Frazer?'

'There now, Harry!' Carol whipped the sheeting away expertly and Harry sat up to examine himself with loving care in the mirror. Then she crossed to a basin to wash her hands. A little irritating smile touched her lips as she tore off a paper towel and dried her fingers carefully. 'Rumours and gossip abound in a make-up room, Inspector. People tend to let their hair down here. The only trouble is you can't rely on anything being halfway accurate, let alone true. I wouldn't like to give you any information that might be misleading.'

'Suppose you allow me to be the judge, Miss Frazer,' said Savage dryly.

'Then there is a little matter of loyalty,' Carol went on musingly. 'When people tell me things in here, or I overhear others talking, I regard what they say as confidential.'

Sue marvelled at the inspector's patience, when she herself longed to shake Carol. 'Very well, Miss Frazer! I won't waste my time pressing you. Just one question—when did you last see Sir Hammond Willis?'

'I saw him for a moment this morning, but only in passing,' she replied rather sulkily, thrown out of stride by the unexpected question.

'And before that?'

'Why do you want to know? He called at my flat on Saturday evening for a few minutes. I was just going out with Johnnie—my fiancé, Mr Bexhill!'

'Did you see him yesterday?'

'No, I didn't,' she replied angrily. 'I'd like to know the reason for these questions.'

'Yes, I'm sure you would, Miss Frazer,' he agreed politely. 'Actually you have been more helpful than you intended to be.'

'I didn't intend—' Carol began, caught off guard.

'I realise that, Miss Frazer,' said Savage pleasantly, and moved to the door. Sue paused only to give her a pithy account of her manners and her crass stupidity in trying to be clever with the police, then followed. Even had she remembered Johnnie Bexhill's message, she would have been in no mood to deliver it with tact.

Outside in the corridor, she apologised for Carol's behaviour, explaining awkwardly: 'She's only young and brash, in spite of her sophisticated appearance.'

Savage acknowledged the remark with a curt nod and accompanied her absently towards Rianne's dressing-room. He did not speak until Sue opened a door which bore a star and had Rianne's name painted underneath.

'This quarrel Miss Frazer had with Lady Willis. Was it on account of Sir Hammond?'

Sue crossed the room and picked up the bundle of envelopes from the dressing-table, shuffling through them nervously. 'I haven't heard Lylah's version but I understand she and Carol never hit it off. It's a complicated story. When Lylah's mother died, her father married again—a pretty girl who left him shortly after their daughter Carol was born. Despite this—or because of it—Mr Frazer doted on Carol which must have hurt Lylah badly. When he died, by which time Lylah was married to Sir Hammond, he asked Lylah to look after Carol, who was the dead image of her mother in looks as well as temperament.

'Whether Lylah felt that Carol was as flighty as her mother, and might take her husband away, I don't know. Lylah threw Carol out of her home because Sir Hammond was becoming too interested. I understand he paid for Carol's trip to America and her training over there, and has also made himself responsible for the rent of her flat. Perhaps he feels somewhat to blame for the rift between Lylah and Carol.'

'Does Miss Frazer's fiancé know all this?'

'I suppose Johnnie knows. Carol has never made a secret of her stepbrother-in-law's favours.'

'You said earlier that Miss May snubbed Carol. Was there jealousy between them because of Sir Hammond? Did Carol resent his newer interest?'

'I don't precisely know. As far as Rianne was concerned the snub was designed merely to put Carol in her place. She gets a bit brash as you saw just now. I don't think there was—' Sue broke off abruptly, her eyes riveted on the letter she had accidentally shuffled to the top of the bundle.

'Mr Savage!' she said in a small, frightened voice. 'This could be another one.'

Savage stepped forward swiftly. 'Another anonymous letter? Don't open it—just give it to me!'

Sue handed it to him with the tips of her fingers. He rummaged through the litter on Rianne's dressing-table and selected a nail file and a pair of tweezers. Slitting the envelope he carefully drew out the contents with the tweezers and spread the letter open.

Sue looked over his shoulder. 'Yes, it's just like the one I burnt— the same cut-out words.' She read the message aloud.

—NEXT TIME THERE WILL BE NO MISTAKE RIANNE MAY

6

'So he is quite convinced that Rianne is hiding. The second letter was posted before the news was published of her disappearance.'

'And it wouldn't have been sent if the writer had intended to abduct Rianne,' agreed Mother Paul. She transferred her gentle gaze from Sue to a print of Da Vinci's *The Last Supper* which had hung in the parlour of Maryhill for as long as the girl could remember. 'So odd! It quite intrigues me!'

Sue took the opportunity of the nun's reverie to have another mouthful of the supper Mother Paul had placed before her. The cheese omelette was fluffy and tasty and piping hot, but she found it disconcerting to eat with a nun looking on. She hadn't realised how hungry she was until she had arrived at Maryhill and Mother Paul, scanning her lovingly, had said: 'Dear child, quite exhausted-looking! You probably haven't eaten all day. So necessary, Sue. You'll only go forgetting things that I'll want to know. Sit down and rest while I get you a little something from the kitchens.'

She pushed the girl gently into one of the big leather armchairs in front of the fire and rustled away. Sue pulled off her gloves wearily and tossed her hat aside. Then she leant her head against the arm of the chair and stared into the flames. It had been quite a day, ending with an irritating session with Lylah Willis who had come to the studio in search of her.

Sir Hammond's hostile secretary had been sent to collect her just as Sue was packing up to go home to the flat. Savage had left earlier, saying goodbye to the girl in the reception foyer where their tour had ended. 'Tell Sir Hammond I'll be watching the *Rianne May Show* this evening with great interest,' he told Sue smoothly, when she hinted that Sir Hammond probably expected some sort of report before he left. 'And convey my thanks for his co-operation. I've appreciated yours, too, Miss Berry. I'll keep in touch with you regarding Miss May. In the meantime, should you think or learn of anything that might lead to her whereabouts, don't hesitate to call that number I gave you. You have it still?'

Sue nodded, then said timidly as he seemed anxious to be gone: 'Mother Paul would like to see you, Inspector. She called me early this morning.'

His face lit up momentarily as though the mention of the nun's name was a solace. Then he glanced at his watch and frowned. 'Tell her I'll be along as soon as I can. In a day or two, perhaps. She probably wants to know how that poor dead girl's parents reacted. It was most distressing—too distressing to talk about yet. Poor devils: they were devoted to the girl.'

Sue did not even have time to express her sympathy. He was gone and she went back to Rianne's dressing-room and began gathering up the papers she had been working on. That was when Sir Hammond's secretary put her head in the door. 'Oh, there you are! I've been looking everywhere for you. I've already called this extension three times.'

'Sorry,' said Sue. 'I've been out of the room.'

'So I gathered—running round with that policeman, they tell me. I saw you together in the canteen. Where is he? Sir Hammond wants to see him.'

'He's gone.'

'Oh, but he can't have! Didn't he know Sir Hammond would want a report?'

'I'm quite sure the inspector will be making a report as soon as possible. He probably had work to do in his own office.'

'Well, I don't know what Sir Hammond will say to this. But you'd better come along instead. Anyway, Lady Willis did say she wanted to see you. She's with Sir Hammond now.'

Sue finished packing the papers into the pigskin briefcase that Rianne had given her—one of the many presents she had thrown casually at her secretary—and picked up her hat and gloves. If she had to see Lylah, she was going to make it quite clear that she was on her way home.

Lady Willis, in overwhelming furs and a hat like a horticultural display, was in no pleasant mood. Sue wondered if husband and wife had been quarrelling, the atmosphere was so tense. They had been standing at either end of the room and Sir Hammond had turned away as Sue entered.

'So, there you are, Suzanne,' exclaimed Lylah effusively which instantly put Sue on her guard. Any sign of graciousness on Lady Willis's part always meant that she wanted something. 'I expected to see you this morning. I asked you to come and see me, remember? My husband has been telling me you've become quite intimate with that inspector who came to Maryhill yesterday.'

Sir Hammond said in the tone of weary humour he always used when speaking to his wife: 'I told you nothing of the sort, my dear. Miss Berry has merely been showing Inspector Savage round the studio on my directions.'

'What did you want to see me about, Lylah?' Sue asked, standing just inside the door. 'I was just leaving.'

'Well, I'm sure you're in no hurry now that Rianne isn't there demanding your attention. You must be glad of the break, my dear Sue. Now about the position of treasurer—you'll have to collect all the stuff Moya had at Maryhill yesterday, which was left behind in all the excitement. Small wonder. I've already contacted Mother Paul and she has it put aside. I said you'd call in this evening to pick it up. Carol may have some of the ledgers also, I don't know—she wasn't much of an assistant to Moya. Bone lazy and quite irresponsible, so I daresay poor Moya had to do the bulk of the work. In fact, I welcome this opportunity to remove Carol from the executive. Unless you are prepared to give her another chance, Sue?'

'Lylah, I'm sorry but I don't want the job. But I don't mind collecting the material for you as I'm going along to see Mother Paul this evening. Shall I hand them to Carol tomorrow?'

Lady Willis's eyes bulged incredulously. 'My dear Sue, you don't seem to realise the compliment that has been paid you. It's not often I select someone out of the blue, as it were. Even Janet—and you know how difficult and stubborn she can be on occasions—agreed that you would be well suited to the job. In fact, out of all the committee only Eunice made any demur, but you needn't let that worry you, my dear! Lady Willis examined her flashing array of rings and gave a little deprecatory laugh. 'She's so devoted to me that she's inclined to get jealous of anyone I favour, foolish girl! I absolutely insist upon your accepting the position, Sue.'

'Oh, all right, then, Lylah,' agreed Sue, almost too tired to argue. It was like Lylah Willis to bother over such little matters which gave her authority. The fact that Moya had been murdered and Rianne was missing seemed to have had no effect on her at all. 'But don't expect too much—my job with Rianne doesn't give me a great deal of spare time.'

'Time?' echoed Lylah. 'Do you know the number of committees I serve on? And what work have you got to do now that Rianne has gone?'

'I'm hoping she'll soon be back,' said Sue steadily. 'Aren't you, Lylah?'

But Lady Willis ignored the question and addressed her husband: 'Are you coming, Hammond? The Greswicks are dining with us to-night, remember?'

'Presently, my dear. You go along. I want to make some arrangements about Rianne's flat and car with Miss Berry.' He opened the door with a flourish that was, in itself, a faint mockery. After a brief hesitation, Lylah was compelled to leave.

Sir Hammond shut the door after her firmly. Then he looked at Sue with the expression of false geniality that she always mistrusted. 'You knew my wife at school, didn't you? Was she the same then?'

'Lylah was in a higher class. I didn't know her very well,' Sue replied briefly. 'What do you want done about the flat and the car, Sir Hammond?'

'Nothing. I was merely using them as an excuse. Somehow, mention of the police seems to upset my wife, and I was wanting to know what progress Inspector Savage had made. What sinister facts has he uncovered about my staff?'

Sue became even more wary. 'He had to leave in a hurry, but he gave me a message—that he would be watching the show tonight with great interest.'

Sir Hammond's face hardened. 'Does that mean he has accomplished nothing after spending the day questioning my staff and being allowed a free run of the place?'

Sue said nothing and edged closer to the door, hoping to end the interview. Sir Hammond without his genial mask made her nervous.

'I have an idea, Miss Berry, that the inspector regards me with some suspicion. What do you think?'

'I wouldn't know,' she replied, trying to sound casual.

'Oh, come now, Miss Berry,' he exclaimed with a laugh. 'You've been with him all day and you're a smart girl. You must have some idea of the lines he's working along, surely.'

'I know nothing of police procedure. Inspector Savage questioned numerous people but I have no idea whom he suspects.' Sue paused for a moment, then added with more assurance: 'But he does seem certain that Rianne is hiding somewhere. There was another anonymous letter in her mail this morning—obviously posted before her disappearance was made known.'

He seemed startled at that piece of news, but recovered himself quickly. 'Indeed? That's interesting, very interesting! Has Savage any idea who is responsible for these letters?'

Sue regarded him steadily. 'Well, one thing is certain—he can hardly suspect you. You knew that Rianne had disappeared. And so did Carol.'

'Carol!' he echoed impatiently. 'She's got nothing to do with this. Who told you she knew about Rianne's disappearance?'

'Johnnie Bexhill. He saw Carol last night.'

'Does Savage think I told Carol?' demanded Sir Hammond haughtily. 'After giving him my word? Why, I didn't even mention the matter to my own—' he stopped, then added quickly: 'I think the point is being laboured. It doesn't seem of much importance to me.'

When Sue repeated this conversation later to Mother Paul, the nun exclaimed softly: 'Ah! But it is those seemingly unimportant points that do matter.'

The rattle of delicate bone china aroused Sue. She started up guiltily and found Mother Paul, a tray between her hands, smiling down at her. 'I must have fallen asleep,' Sue said, glancing at her watch in surprise. Nearly an hour had passed.

'I always like to wait until Sister goes to her prayers,' explained the nun apologetically, as though she made a habit of raiding the larder. 'So distracting having me poking through her domain. Never test a nun's virtues if their duties are either cooking or teaching music. Such temperamental vocations.'

Sue laughed as she took the tray on to her lap. 'I wish I were back at Maryhill,' she confessed.

Mother Paul, seating herself in a straight chair opposite, blinked in surprise. 'Do you, dear? How very strange you should say that!'

Sue tried to control the wobble in her voice: 'I feel so secure here, so safe, instead of being involved in the murky mess of other people's lives.'

'Yes, very distressing,' agreed the nun soothingly. 'But you will feel better when you have told me everything that has been happening. Did you see Mr Savage today?'

Sue nodded and swallowed hastily. If Mother Paul wanted her to talk then she would have to remember to take smaller mouthfuls. She gave her Savage's message, omitting his comment about Moya's parents. She had no wish to upset the gentle nun. She added simply that he was very busy.

A little frown creased the smooth forehead under the shadow of the black veil. 'Yes, I know how busy he must be! But it is so necessary to see him in person.' She paused and eyed the girl thoughtfully. 'Such an awkward situation! Will you tell him, Sue, that I would appreciate his calling as soon as possible—and that I'm sure he would not find the time spent unrewarding?'

'Very well, I'll tell him,' Sue promised doubtfully. 'He did say he would keep in touch with me about Rianne.'

'Are you very anxious about her, Sue?' asked the nun earnestly.

'Sometimes,' replied the girl, in a small, tense voice. 'I keep thinking I let her down—that I should have won more of her confidence. In many ways Rianne is very childlike, easily frightened, easily soothed. If only she would come forward I'm sure the inspector would not only be able to help her out of whatever mess she thinks she's in, but also clear up the whole ghastly business. Then I start thinking maybe she can't come forward—that Mr Savage could be wrong and she has been kidnapped, perhaps even—even murdered!'

Mother Paul put a swift, light hand on the girl's lips. 'You mustn't even think like that, Sue. Rianne is alive and well. I know Mr Savage — he doesn't arrive at a conclusion until he is quite, quite sure.'

The girl relaxed and tried to smile. 'I told you I wished I were back here.'

'You are back at Maryhill at the moment and I am ready to listen — just like the old days. I want you to tell me about the people at the studio, how they are connected with Rianne and what questions Mr Savage asked. Don't omit even the smallest detail — it could well be the largest clue.' It was a relief to pour out the irritating and uneasy events of the day to such an attentive listener. By the time her recital had finished, Sue had revived enough to say with mock despair: 'And to cap it all, I've allowed Lylah Willis to push me on to her committee of Maryhill Past Students. She said I was to collect some books and papers from you.'

'Yes, I have them safe,' Mother Paul said with a nod. 'That is, such as I could find. So much confusion that dreadful day!' She fumbled under her scapular and brought out a watch on a length of black cord. 'Nearly time for the *Rianne May Show*. I'm allowing the senior boarders to watch it, too. We put the convent set into their recreation room. Perhaps you'd like to stay for it, Sue?'

'Yes, I want to see it. Sir Hammond is hoping for big things.'

'You remember where the girls' room is? I'll just slip down to the kitchen with the tray and will join you there presently.'

Sue helped pack the dishes and held open the door for the nun to pass through. Then she made her way slowly towards the once familiar room, smiling in reminiscence. When she had been at Maryhill it had been the radio blaring or someone thumping on the piano while the girls practised dance steps together. Now they all sat in a silent circle in the semi-darkness watching a small screen.

But the television set had not been switched on and the perennial schoolgirl sounds of much chattering and giggling still came from the recreation room. Both broke off abruptly when Sue opened the door and the faces that turned towards her became politely guarded.

'I didn't mean to interrupt anything,' said Sue, feeling old and awkward. 'Mother Paul said you are going to watch the *Rianne May Show*. I hope you don't mind if I crash in on the party.'

No one answered and Sue recalled herself at the same age when a visitor appeared unexpectedly, with no one liking to take the lead in replying, yet giggling and mimicking the stranger after she had gone. She realised uncomfortably now that the bright, over-loud voice visitors had used had been pure nervousness at being confronted by a group of schoolgirls secure in their bulk anonymity.

'Why, hello, Sandra!' Sue recognized Lylah Willis's daughter with a gratitude for which she despised herself but could not help.

The girl muttered a reply and glanced sideways at the others, obviously disliking having been singled out. 'Oh, and Jillian, too!' She hastened to rectify her mistake. 'How is your mother, Jill?'

'She's all right, thank you,' replied Jillian Hurley, staring at Sue as though she were quite deranged.

'Yes, well, uh, look, can't we all sit down?' suggested Sue heartily. 'You make me feel incredibly old standing up like that. Let's relax, shall we? I suppose you've been discussing Rianne May's disappearance. Has anyone come up with a bright idea? If so, tonight's your chance. The show has been made into a special edition appealing for information. Anyone who thinks they may be able to help can ring the studio.'

Oh, dear, perhaps I shouldn't have said that, she thought. *Mother Paul will bless me if they start to riot.*

Much to her relief they suddenly rose again as a file of nuns came in and took up the front row of chairs that had been arranged in a semi-circle in front of the television set. Then Mother Paul rustled in swiftly. 'Sue, dear, will you switch it on? So good to have an expert— sometimes it blinks! Jillian, the overhead lights—just leave one of the wall brackets.'

Sue fiddled with the controls long enough to justify Mother Paul's faith in her as an expert. 'That's beautiful dear,' called the nun. 'Now come and sit down next to me.

'Yes, Sister?' She turned her head as one of the nuns bent close and murmured against her veil.

Sue, removing the satchel which was marked M.C. from the chair next to Mother Paul, overheard her reply. 'Well, just avert your gaze, Sister. Goodness me, weren't we trained enough in the custody of the eyes when we were novices?'

'Are these the M.P.S.A. papers?' asked Sue.

Mother Paul nodded, then whispered confidentially: 'Poor Sister Julian. She's worried about the girls, too! Some of the advertisements with ladies having baths so as to sell soap. Do you think, Sue, that you could pretend to make some adjustment to the picture?'

Sue bit her lip and stared hard at the prosaic test pattern. 'The show is going to be run without any commercials. I don't think there will be anything in the least objectionable.' She ran a mental eye over the ballet costumes and decided they would pass—just! No low comedy sequence tonight, thank goodness! Unless Roger Petrie had included one of Rianne's sketches, but it wouldn't be like him to strike a false note.

The show opened with every still of Rianne the studio could lay hands on being flashed rapidly one after the other on the screen. Rianne in every attitude, from every angle, in every mood—glamorous studio poses, engaging off-camera shots, stills frozen from items in past shows in glittering, extravagant gowns that she had had made by top European couturiers especially for television, in tights and leotard with a scarf tying back her gleaming hair as she limbered up at a barre, in a Merry Widow hat and a feather boa and a gown of the nineties so low cut that it was almost out of camera range. The accompanying sound consisted of a glamorous and gay pot-pourri that the musical director had made out of every song and dance piece that Rianne had ever used.

Then, just when you felt you couldn't bear to see another shot of the same face or hear another note of the ringing music, both were broken off abruptly. There was a singing quality in the silence that followed as the camera focused steadily on the huge archway where Rianne usually appeared in curvaceous silhouette at the opening of the show. Slowly, as though from a long distance, the camera glided to a close-up of the lighted and empty archway and a quiet, even voice—Sue recognised it as the terribly sincere tones of the studio's star news commentator—said: 'Rianne May! Where is Rianne May?'

'Clever!' murmured Mother Paul. 'Dear me, what an immense place it must be!'

'Not really,' Sue whispered back. 'The lighting and camera work combine to create an illusion of space. Actually there's a rough wall behind that archway only a foot or so away. Rianne used to complain about catching her frocks on it.'

'How odd!' said the nun softly. 'An illusion of space and grandeur.'

'The camera man, Greg Oliphant, is very skilled. You'll see him in a moment. Sir Hammond is going to introduce the people who work behind the scenes on Rianne's show. They are going to form a panel and what they discuss about Rianne is supposed to help viewers suggest where she might be—or what might have happened to her,' added Sue in an unhappy voice.

Sir Hammond's distinguished head and shoulders filled the screen, his eyes grave and direct. There was movement and subdued giggling among the boarders as they turned to Sandra Willis. To have such a famous father was really something to be proud of.

'This part of the show was taped this afternoon,' explained Sue.

'Taped?' The nun echoed.

'Filmed like an ordinary moving picture. Then the advance segments are set up on a special camera so that all Roger has to do—he's the director-producer—is press a button.'

'You mean that they are not talking together about Rianne now—at this moment? Does everyone know of this . . . this deception?'

'Pre-recording certain segments is quite a common practice. It's the usual way for a big show to be put together. Viewers are probably aware that some parts of it are not going on at their precise moment of watching, but they don't allow the knowledge to spoil the show.'

'It seems that a number of aspects of television are not what they appear to be,' observed the nun, a note of wonder in her voice. Presently she touched the girl's hand warmly. 'You have been most informative, Sue dear. Such a help!'

'What do you mean, Mother Paul?'

'Not now—we must be disturbing the others who want to hear what is being said. Such young men—and one of them so good-looking!'

'That's Roger Petrie,' said Sue, rather self-consciously.

'I like the other one's eyes better,' remarked the nun, after a pause. 'Such an honest look. Why isn't he on the panel?'

'Which other one?' asked Sue, puzzled.

'The young man who was supposed to look after Rianne. I do

hope he didn't lose his job. I'm sure Rianne wouldn't like that.'

'Oh, you mean Ted Brown. He and the other security guards are manning special telephones to take calls from viewers.'

'Oh, dear, it all sounds so exciting. Poor Mr Savage—so courteous and patient always!'

'He showed the greatest dislike for Sir Hammond's scheme,' admitted Sue, 'but there was nothing he could do about it. Then Sir Hammond offered to take all the calls so that he wouldn't be annoyed by cranks.'

'That was quite wrong, too,' said Mother Paul regretfully. 'How can an untrained person like Sir Hammond possibly know which are the genuine cranks. For you must know, Sue dear, that even some of the oddest sounding information could contain a grain of truth. So trying for Mr Savage when it's people who are withholding information that he wants to hear from, not the ones who are over-ready with it. Would you try to impress upon him I'm not one of them, Sue?'

Sue nodded distractedly. Her attention wandered in a no-man's-land, unfixed either by the screen or the significance of Mother Paul's remarks.

'Some people withhold information on purpose,' went on the nun pensively, 'but others withhold it unwittingly.'

Sue nodded towards the screen. 'These are some of the people Inspector Savage interviewed today. Comparing their remarks with what I told you about their replies to him, what would you say? Are they withholding information wittingly or not?'

The nun was silent and they listened to some of the theories being put forward concerning Rianne. Then Sue said apologetically. 'They have to dramatize a bit. After all, it is a show they are running.'

Mother Paul gripped her hand suddenly. 'Precisely, dear child! I daresay each one has something to hide, but that is not as misleading as unwittingly adding to an illusion—which is what is actually happening in this absurd charade. Do you follow what I mean, Sue?'

'No,' replied the girl despairingly.

'Then I'll try to explain . . .'

But the nun's explanation was not to be given until some time later, while the events that followed her abrupt pause put the whispered, enigmatic remarks in front of the school television set completely out of Sue's mind.

From the back of the darkened room came the high, quavering voice of one of the girls: 'Mother Paul! There's a strange man in the room!'

7

Heads turned swiftly. 'Who called out?' asked Mother Paul sharply, rising from her chair and facing the room.

'He's over here . . . behind the bookcase,' replied the same voice, even more tremulously.

'Sue, the lights!'

Sue moved quickly towards the switches near the door.

'No! No lights!' said a man's voice. 'Don't move any of you, I'm armed!'

One of the girls screamed and Sue pulled herself up, the nausea of fear rising in her throat.

'Hush! Be quiet!' commanded Mother Paul sternly, as other cries went up and the girls huddled together, sobbing. 'No one is to make another sound. You, man! Who are you and what do you want here? Answer me quickly before I call the police!'

'No police, I'm armed,' repeated the unseen intruder. It was a strangely toneless voice, overlaid with weariness. 'I won't hurt anyone. I just want to talk. But no police—I'm armed.'

'So you've said,' replied Mother Paul, rather tartly. 'You ought to be ashamed of yourself, frightening women and children.'

'Stand back, Sister! Keep away from me. Look! See this knife?' The man stepped forward from the shadow of the bookcase, and Sue, closer to him than the nun, saw an ugly flash of steel in the half-light.

Mother Paul paused, but she inclined her head forward and from under the deeper shadow of her veil her eyes gazed at him searchingly. 'How did you get in?' she asked quietly.

'It wasn't hard,' replied the man, responding to the strangely coaxing note in the nun's voice. 'There was a tree—and an open up-stairs window. I'm still pretty fit physically. They encourage me to keep fit, you know.'

'An excellent idea!' said the nun softly. 'Mens sana in corpore—'

'Stop it!' said the stranger harshly. The note of fury in his voice made them all quail. 'You're supposed to be a good woman. Why do you try to provoke me then? I don't want to do you any harm, but don't push me—do you hear?'

'Yes, I hear,' replied Mother Paul, her tone still gently conversa-tional. 'You're not really a burglar, are you? I can see that. Why did you come here? Is there someone special you wanted to talk to?'

The man did not reply. He looked round at the staring, frightened faces vaguely. Then he fastened his eyes on Sue. He gestured at her with the knife, and she tried not to flinch. 'Who are you?' he asked, his eyes sombre and brooding. He blinked them a lot, as though forc-ing himself to focus and be on the alert.

The girl moistened her lips. 'Sue Berry,' she replied, barely above a whisper.

'You're a nurse? You look like a nurse.'

'No, she's not a nurse,' intervened Mother Paul. 'Come, do put down that horrid-looking knife! You're not going to harm us, and we are not going to harm you. Just tell us what you want and then you must go. We can't have strange soldiers wandering round our convent, you know. What if Mother Provincial should hear about your being here!'

'I'll kill you if you betray me!' exclaimed the stranger. 'I'll kill all of you rather than go through it again!'

The desperation and ferocity of his voice silenced even the in-domitable Mother Paul. Out of the corner of her eye, Sue saw the nun's fingers tremble on the long, wooden rosary beads that hung from her leather cincture.

The man shook his head as though to clear it, and said more quiet-ly: 'I get mixed up. Things keep coming back to me—like getting away tonight. I keep remembering other times. It was your fault, reminding me I was a soldier. You shouldn't have done that. Why did you?'

'I'm sorry if I made a mistake,' said Mother Paul, her voice not quite steady. 'I noticed your khaki trousers. Where are you from?'

'Don't keep asking questions,' he answered peevishly. 'You know I can't tell you that. You're only trying to confuse me, so don't keep talking at me. I'm here to do the talking.'

'Very well,' said the nun peaceably. 'Would you mind if I turned off the television? Then we could hear you better. May I?'

He did not answer for a moment. His brooding gaze was caught by a startling close-up of Rianne singing one of her husky, alluring numbers. Staring straight into the camera lens, she seemed to be looking at every person in the room individually. Sue heard him mutter: 'She's beautiful, so beautiful! She mustn't die!'

Sue's already fast-beating heart gave a lurch. 'You know Rianne May? You know where she is?' she managed to bring out.

His eyes slid back to her. 'Which one are you? I don't remember seeing you before.'

'I'm Rianne May's secretary. Where is Rianne? Please tell me!'

'Turn off that row!' He used the knife again to point at the television set. 'You're trying to confuse me again. Lights and noise—I don't know which it was that did for me. And then the silence! Awful silence—but you knew they wouldn't let you sleep. No sleep and just a sip of water—I don't know which it was that did for me.'

Sue tried to be brave like the nun, whom she could see gliding like a shadow along the wall behind the girls. She edged round so that the man, in order to face her, would have his back almost turned on Mother Paul. 'Please!' she begged him again. 'Where is Rianne? You know you can trust me.'

'Which one are you? Did I give it to you? It's very difficult remembering faces, but I'm sure it wasn't you. What's more, I did recognise her face. Are you a friend of hers, too?'

'Yes, I am a friend, a very close friend. We are all her friends here. So if you know anything about her, won't you please tell us?'

'I won't tell you anything, do you hear?' his voice rose again, and Sue could see beads of perspiration on his forehead.

Mother Paul was closer to them now. But the way to the door lay beyond them. When the man made as if to turn, she shrank swiftly behind a pedestal which supported a small and hideous statue of some obscure saint.

'No, you needn't tell me anything,' said Sue, trying to control her voice. 'You may do as you wish. Come, won't you sit down? You look so tired. Perhaps if you rested a little, you'd remember what you came about.'

The man seemed to hesitate. Then he took a step or two forward. 'Where would you like to sit?' asked Sue coaxingly, her eyes never leaving his face. It was a terrific effort to stand still as he came nearer. At any moment she felt her nerves would shatter and she would start screaming in terror. She watched the man's eyes. They were dazed like those of a sleepwalker. 'Come!' she invited again, with all the persuasion she could put into her voice.

Suddenly he stopped and his eyes came alive once more with a flash of fear. 'I know who you are. They tried that, too. You thought they were being kind, but it was just another trick they had. You're one of them. You can't bluff me. I know and I'll—!'

'Mother Paul!' screamed Sue, as he lifted his knife. Her knees crumpled under her and she covered her head instinctively with her arms. There was a thud and a crash, and Sue was knocked sideways as the man sprawled beside her.

'Quickly, someone! Get that knife!' ordered Mother Paul.

Sue, crouched on the floor, gazed fascinated at the trickle of blood curling down the man's forehead.

Mother Paul bent over him. 'Oh, dear, I hope I haven't killed the poor fellow. So odd!'

'Odd?' Sue gave a hysterical laugh as she struggled to her feet. 'A raving lunatic.'

'Yes, dear. I didn't mean that, but no time now to explain. Mother Celestine, go quickly and ring the police. And some of you girls — your belts. Take them off and give them to me. We must confine this poor creature before he revives.'

'Oh, Mother Superior!' exclaimed one of the younger nuns in tearful wonder. 'You held up the statue of St. Thalburga and at the sight of it he fell down unconscious. I shall always pray to her from now on for special protection against intruders.'

'Nonsense, Sister!' replied Mother Paul tartly, tying the man's hands behind his back. 'The only miracle the statue worked was being to hand when I wanted something to knock the poor crazy man out. Have I broken it?'

'A hand was knocked off.' Sue held up a cluster of mauve-coloured fingers pressed gorily round the stems of three plaster roses of improbable hue.

'Damaged beyond repair, thank Heaven!' pronounced Mother Paul. 'Quite hideous! Sue dear, are you all right? Such a shocking experience for everyone. Where is Sister Martha? Oh, Sister—I want you to make cocoa for the girls. Serve it with some of that delicious-looking orange cake I saw in the larder. File down quietly to the refectory like good children—the unpleasantness is over now!'

The man at her feet stirred and groaned. 'Quickly everyone—out! And as soon as you have had supper, go to bed.' Hiding the figure on the floor behind her wide skirts, Mother Paul urged the boarders and nuns out of the room.

Mother Celestine appeared on the threshold as the last one vanished. 'Mother Superior, I didn't have to call the police. They were already at the front door wanting permission to search our grounds. Another man is with them. He says he's a nurse from the Wesburn Repatriation Hospital. They're looking for a . . . a mentally deranged patient.'

'Ah, yes, just as we thought. Poor frightened fellow, so confused! I wonder if he'll be able to tell us what brought him here?'

'It was something to do with Rianne,' said Sue. 'I'm sure of that.'

Two uniformed policemen and a burly individual, wearing a white coat and carrying a bag, came quickly into the room.

'Is this the man?' one of the policemen asked the attendant as he dropped to a knee beside the figure on the floor. He nodded and opened his bag.

'How did he hurt his head?' he demanded accusingly.

'I'm afraid I did that,' confessed Mother Paul meekly. 'He was threatening us with a knife. Of course I realise he was not responsible, but—'

'Aggressive, was he? I'd better give him a shot then.' The male nurse took out a hypodermic and filled it carefully.

'Must you?' inquired the nun. 'I rather wanted to ask him . . . ' then she paused.

'Ask him what?' said one of the policemen keenly.

'To forgive me for striking him,' replied Mother Paul innocently.

'That's all right, Sister,' said the male nurse. 'If you had to, you had to! They all have these bouts, you know, when they either want to hurt someone or themselves.'

'Ah, poor soul!' exclaimed Mother Paul compassionately.

'Don't take it to heart, Sister. Most times he's pretty happy, aren't you, George? Are you awake then? Do you know me? I've come to take you home, old chap. You had us real worried, nicking off like that. Have you got anything for me, huh?' The nurse felt him all over, saying in an aside: 'As a rule he's a good boy—always lets you know when he feels a bout coming on and hands over anything he's collected that might do some damage.'

'You mean—like this knife?' asked Sue, giving it up thankfully.

The policeman examined it. 'Just as well we weren't far behind,' one remarked. 'We'd had a report that he'd been seen in this vicinity. Shall we go now? I don't suppose you want to make a charge or anything like that, Sister?'

'Indeed, no!' replied the nun quickly.

'Come on, Georgie boy. Upsadaisy!'

The nurse, assisted by one of the policemen, hauled the intruder to his feet, where he hung like a stuffed doll between them, the sedative taking over from where Mother Paul left off.

'Has he family? Friends?' The nun seemed oddly reluctant to let him go. 'I'd like to explain to them what happened.'

'Don't think he has any people. You could try Records, of course, but I can't rightly recall his ever having visitors other than Red Cross folk.'

'Perhaps one of the sisters and I could come and see him,' offered Mother Paul.

'That's good of you, Sister. Leave it for a bit though. The doctors usually sedate him for a few days after a bout. All right now, Georgie, old chap—about turn!'

'Just one moment!' said the nun. She reached out her hand and put it on the man's now flaccid arm. 'I'll come and see you,' she promised, looking into his dull eyes. 'And we'll have a nice long talk. What would you like to talk about? Books, music, perhaps television, and Rianne May?'

'Rianne May!' exclaimed the policeman sharply. 'That's the TV star who's missing. He wouldn't know anything about her, would he?'

'Oh, wouldn't he!' said the male nurse. 'You don't know Georgie. Rianne's the latest pin-up in his ward. They've got their own telly. They were real upset when they read about her nearly being killed. Come on, I'd better get him back right away, if it's all the same to you. Good night. Sister, and you, er, Miss. Sorry you had such a fright. All right, George me boy, left, right, left, right. At the double!'

'Pin-up!' repeated Mother Paul in a puzzled voice to Mother Celestine and Sue, as they watched from the front door the men bundling George into the police car.

'People cut out photographs of their favourite stars from papers and magazines and pin them up where they can see them,' explained Mother Celestine, not without a trace of pride in her worldly knowledge. 'Evidently Rianne must be—' she broke off, gasped audibly, and in a trembling voice invoked St. Thalburga, that newly appointed protectress from intruders.

Barely had the four strange men driven off in a dramatic sweep of gravel than another masculine shape came into the shaft of light thrown through the open front door.

'Dear me!' Mother Paul observed mildly. 'You'd never think this was a secluded retreat for female religious.'

'It's Ted,' said Sue. 'Don't be worried, Mother Celestine, I know this man. He's a security officer from the studio.'

'Do come in, Mr Brown,' Mother Paul invited warmly, as Ted, one foot on the lowest stone step, looked up at them.

'Mother Superior!' exclaimed her sister-in-religion faintly. 'I wonder if you would allow me to retire?'

'Of course, Mother Celestine,' replied the other tenderly. 'Far too many strange men for one night. And just look at our parquet floor. As if it's not enough to have poor Father Maher always forgetting to wipe his shoes.'

Ted hastily rubbed his feet on the mat before stepping over the threshold.

'Did you come to pick me up, Ted?' asked Sue, appreciative but puzzled. 'I thought you were supposed to be handling calls from the show.'

'Did you get many?' asked Mother Paul. 'Poor Mr Savage!'

'There were a few. I left the other chaps to take over.' He glanced from Sue to the nun and then over his shoulder. 'Wasn't that a police car?'

'Such an extraordinary evening—quite terrifying!' exclaimed Mother Paul and gave him a summary of what had happened.

Sue, watching his enigmatic expression, felt ashamed of herself for wishing he would not appear too unconcerned to Mother Paul, although why she should want him to make an impression she could not fathom. When the nun, looking up at him trustfully, asked: 'Now what do you make of this odd affair?' Sue broke in with her own opinion. This had been somewhat revised following the male nurse's remarks.

'I don't suppose the escaped patient knew anything about Rianne after all. How could he, if he's in that hospital all the time and, when he does get out, they go after him pretty smartly? But people—even normal people—often feel they know Rianne personally after seeing her on television. She has that special gift of being able to project herself individually, if you can follow what I mean.

'In my opinion, the poor fellow, through reading the account of the murder and Rianne's disappearance in the papers, evolved some confused, romantic rescue plan in his head which brought him to the place where the murder attempt was made. I can't see his being here as anything more than a coincidence.'

Mother Paul inclined her head slowly. 'Is that what you think, too, Mr Brown?'

Ted smiled at her and then looked shyly across at Sue, 'I guess Sue knows what she's talking about. We had some pretty queer phone calls, too. There are more out than in, if you ask me. Did you watch the show, Sue?

'We were in the middle of it when our lunatic broke in.

'Did everyone see it? Sir Hammond's girl and all?

'Sandra Willis?' said Mother Paul, in a soft enquiring voice. 'Yes, she was amongst the girls. But why do you ask, Mr Brown?'

'I just thought Sir Hammond would like to know,' he returned, meeting her gaze with candid eyes.

Mother Paul considered him thoughtfully for a moment. Then

she said: 'So kind of you to come and fetch Sue. Have you got those tedious treasurer papers, dear child? I wish you would check that they are all there as soon as you can. Lylah will be on the telephone making sure I gave them to you. But that won't be the real reason, of course.' She leant forward and embraced Sue fondly. 'You will tell Mr Savage to come, won't you? So important! Goodbye, Mr Brown! I know I can rely on you to take great care of Sue. You must come and see me when all the stress is over and tell me if I was not undeceived.'

'Whatever did that nun of yours mean?' asked Ted as they drove down the long driveway and through the gates.

Sue, who had been about to ask him the same question, said wearily: 'How should I know? Perhaps she thinks that, because you're a security officer, you should be a lot smarter than you are. Oh, Ted, I'm sorry! That was a beastly thing to say. I always seem to get nasty after being frightened half to death.'

'I wasn't so smart letting Rianne get away like that.' But he seemed to be speaking to himself, rather than brushing aside her apology.

Sue had not expected to see Inspector Savage so soon as the following morning. But he was getting out of his car as she and Ted swept into the bay marked with Rianne's name in the studio parking lot. He strolled across to them, eyeing the Mercedes rather quizzically.

Sue smiled in a deprecatory way. 'Sir Hammond said to carry on just as if Rianne were here.'

'And why not?' he agreed. 'You're probably saving him income tax. Good morning, Brown.'

'Good morning, Inspector,' replied Ted, handing Sue her briefcase.

'Thank you,' she said. 'All the same, Ted, I don't think we should overdo it. Didn't I hear you go out again last night after you brought me home from Maryhill?'

'I slipped out to see my mother,' he admitted promptly.

'For Pete's sake, where does she live? You clocked up over fifty miles. Take it easy, or Sir Hammond might change his mind.'

'Yes, it was a bit much,' he confessed guiltily. 'And Mother wasn't in, either.'

'That was bad luck,' remarked Savage genially. 'A trip into the country for nothing. But I daresay you felt you had to go. Are you coming in, Miss Berry?'

They left Ted and crossed together to the studio building. 'Inspector,' said Sue suddenly, 'I suppose you've checked on all of us?'

'What do you mean, Miss Berry?'

'I know you must have gone into the backgrounds of the studio personnel. What about mine and — and Ted's?'

Savage paused, eyeing her thoughtfully. 'He's always worried you a bit, hasn't he? As a matter of fact, I did check on him. There's nothing in his background that suggests any unlawful activities.'

'No, of course not,' said Sue quickly. 'I didn't mean . . . I just thought someone might be . . . well, using him. I sometimes feel that he's got an . . . an ulterior motive in everything.'

'What you say sounds interesting but rather vague, Miss Berry.'

The girl took a deep breath. 'What I'm trying to say is that you can't hold anything against Ted if . . . if he's only doing what someone else tells him as . . . well, as part of his job.'

Savage paused again. The lurking twinkle had left his eyes when he spoke. 'If Ted or anyone else knows Rianne's whereabouts and is not making any attempt to inform the police, then I do hold it against them.'

'In that case,' said Sue, trying to speak coolly. 'I'd better tell you about the man who broke into Maryhill last night.'

'The patient who escaped from Wesburn Repatriation Hospital?'

'Oh, you know about him? I might have guessed. One of the policemen who came to collect him pricked up his ears at once when Mother Paul mentioned Rianne's name. Who is the patient? Has he any connections with Rianne?'

'Not as far as we can discover. I'm inclined to lay the blame for his untimely appearance at Sir Hammond's door for putting on that show. I expect quite a few similar cases this morning.'

Sue smiled. 'Mother Paul said: "Poor Mr Savage," when I told her the reasons behind last night's edition. She is still most anxious to see you, by the way.'

He made an abject gesture. 'Just as soon as I can. I understand she was, er, responsible for the man's detention.'

Sue laughed. 'But it wasn't funny at the time, I can tell you.'

'I'm sure it wasn't—not for the unfortunate chap, either. It seems he's been in bad shape ever since the Korean War. He was captured behind the lines and had a pretty rough time of it from the Communists.'

Sue nodded. 'We guessed something of the sort from the way he spoke. Do you want me to let Sir Hammond's secretary know you're here? He may not be in yet, but she'll probably have the list of calls that came in last night.'

'Later. I want to see Mr Watts again. Perhaps you could tell me where to find him?'

Sue glanced at her watch. 'He may be in the post-mortem room. An office near Studio 2 where the production and technical staff get together to discuss a show,' she explained. 'I'll show you the way if you like.'

Roger Petrie opened the door to Sue's knock. 'Why, hello!' but the sudden warmth in his expression vanished when he saw the inspector behind her.

Sue said shyly and apologetically: 'Is Eric with you? Inspector Savage wants to see him.'

'Yes, he's here. We're just in the middle of a conference.'

'Perhaps Mr Watts can be spared for a while,' suggested Savage amiably.

'Who wants me?' demanded an irritable voice. 'Oh, it's that policeman again, is it? I can't talk to anyone. Now, Greg, if you could angle your camera slightly to the left—'

'I'm sorry, Mr Watts,' interrupted Savage, entering the room, 'but I'll have to ask you a few questions.'

'Didn't you ask enough questions yesterday?' asked Watts surlily. 'All right. What is it now?'

Savage glanced at the others. Greg was watching him guardedly, Johnnie Bexhill with his small mouth open in bewilderment. 'We'll step outside if you like, Inspector, said Roger tactfully.

'Like hell you will!' exclaimed Eric, lounging offensively in his chair. 'This is nothing more than police persecution. I want everyone to stay right here to be witnesses. And that goes for Miss Stoolpigeon Berry, too!'

'That's enough, Eric,' said Roger quietly. 'We'll stay if you want us and if the inspector doesn't object.'

'I have no objection,' replied Savage shortly. 'Now, Mr Watts, you denied yesterday having received money from Miss May. Do you still stick to that?'

'I don't see why not. What business is it of yours what Rianne did with her money? You're not persecuting Greg Oliphant because she gave him presents. See that watch he's got on right now? Ask him what he did to earn that from Rianne.'

Greg lurched up. 'Why, you dirty—'

'Johnnie, grab him!' ordered Roger sharply. 'Now look here, Eric, if you re going to continue being obnoxious we shall leave.'

Watts looked at him sneeringly. 'What did Rianne give you? You tried hard enough. Now you're working on her secretary.'

'Mr Watts,' said Savage sternly. 'If you don't pull yourself together, I'll take you to Headquarters to ask my questions.'

'You can't do that. You'd have to arrest me.'

'You're quite right,' said Savage smoothly, and an ominous hush fell on the room. Greg slumped slowly back in his chair and Johnnie automatically released the grip he had on his shoulder. Sue gave a quick nervous glance at Roger and saw his face dark and intent.

Eric passed his tongue round his dry lips. 'What can you arrest me for?'

'What about blackmail, Mr Watts? I have a witness to prove that Rianne May was paying you money. Moreover, I have certain information concerning her personal bank account. If your claim to have nothing to hide is an honest one, then you won't mind allowing me to see your own bank account.'

'No!' exclaimed Watts. 'I mean, why should I? You can't prove anything like blackmail. It's up to Rianne to make a complaint and Rianne's not here.'

'Precisely,' replied Savage crisply, and again had the effect of stilling the room.

'What do you mean?' asked Watts uneasily.

'I put it to you, Mr Watts, that you have been extorting money from Miss May. Suppose she had decided to stop payment and to make that complaint, what would you have done? There is a certain popular misconception that blackmailers never kill the goose that lays the golden eggs. Frequently, however, the victim's secret is no worse than the identity of a blackmailer, and an impasse develops. If you don't stop blackmailing me, I'll go to the police and tell them you're a blackmailer. In other words, the roles of victim and criminal can become switched. Do you follow?'

'No, I don't!' snapped Watts. 'And I deny both extortion and blackmail. You find Rianne and ask her if I ever made her give me money.'

'Perhaps you can tell us where to find her, Mr Watts?'

'How the hell should I know? If you're suggesting Rianne ran away because I'm a blackmailer, then I'd be the last person to know where she is.'

'I'm suggesting, Mr Watts, that Rianne May disappeared because the blackmailer tried to kill a goose that not only had refused to lay any more golden eggs, but intended turning on him.'

'Are you accusing me of attempting to murder Rianne?'

'You've overlooked something, Mr Watts. A woman *was* murdered.' He paused to allow his words to sink in. 'In mistake for Rianne. The identity of the victim is immaterial to the charge.'

'No!' exclaimed Watts hoarsely. 'You're wrong! I didn't . . . I couldn't . . .'

He half-rose, then sat down again and slipped one hand into his pocket. But before his hand reached his mouth, Johnnie Bexhill flung himself across the intervening table.

'What the hell!' Eric's muffled voice rose in fury.

Savage moved swiftly to the other side of the table. 'That pill, please, Mr Watts,' he demanded sternly. 'All right, leave him alone, Mr Bexhill.'

Eric flung a small white tablet on to the table with shaking fingers. 'Just what was all that about?' he demanded, glaring angrily at Johnnie.

Bexhill's face was flaring from energy and embarrassment. 'Sorry, Eric, but I thought . . . Well, you know how they —'

'You damned interfering fool! You've seen me take these indigestion pills a dozen times. Why don't you think up better scripts instead of pretending you're a private eye.' He turned to Savage, who had crushed the tablet and sniffed at it gingerly. 'Well, Inspector? Are you quite satisfied it's not cyanide?'

'I regret the interruption as much as you do,' replied Savage suavely.

'Thrown you off balance, has it?' returned Eric, recovering his sneer. 'What are you going to do now?'

'Ask you again, Mr Watts, why Rianne May paid you sums of money amounting to several hundred pounds.'

Eric looked round the staring, waiting faces. He straightened his tie and shrugged his jacket back into alignment. His long, thin mouth curled triumphantly. 'I still say it's none of your business. I also say that there is no law against a wife handing money to her husband for safe keeping.'

8

The stunned silence in the conference room was broken by Greg Oliphant. 'Rianne married *you*! I don't believe it!'

'Bit of a shock to you, is it?' sneered Watts, stung by the horrified surprise in the young man's voice.

Roger Petrie brushed by Sue to the door. He opened it, looked out, then shut it and stood with his back to it. 'If what you say is true, Eric, then it mustn't go any further than this room. You understand, Greg? Inspector Savage—'

'Yes, Maisie had the same ideas as you have,' said Eric, with an unpleasant grin. 'Bad publicity for a big star to be married—and to a paltry floor manager to boot.'

But Roger was looking fixedly at the inspector. 'This won't have to come out, will it?'

'That depends,' replied Savage cautiously, then he turned to Eric Watts. 'All right, Mr Watts. I take it you have proof of your marriage to Rianne May?'

'Maisie Ryan,' Watts corrected sardonically. 'We married before her meteoric climb to fame and a new name. Caxton Hall in London eight years ago, if you want to check.'

'A registry office!' exclaimed Sue involuntarily. It seemed so unlike the publicity-loving Rianne not to insist on a splash-up wedding with admiring crowds, and once again it struck her that she should have made a greater effort to get beneath Rianne's façade. Did something of the old, uncertain Maisie Ryan still exist? How badly had she needed help?

'For how long did you and Rianne live together as man and wife?' the inspector was saying.

Watts eyed him guardedly. 'A year or so, on and off, if you know what I mean. We split up finally after three years. Maisie had never been what you might call an easy woman to live with. And, frankly, it was a relief when she cleared out for good. I came out here then.'

'The decision to part was by mutual agreement?'

'I suppose you could say that, yes.'

'Then why did Miss May give you money when she met you again as a stranger after a period of . . . five years, is it?'

'We're still husband and wife,' declared Watts defiantly.

'And you threatened to expose your marriage?'

'Well, I did sort of drop a hint that her Australian public mightn't take kindly to the news,' acknowledged Watts slyly. 'But we never discussed terms or anything, so you can hardly call it blackmail.'

'Then what did you discuss, Mr Watts? Some other information perhaps? Something Rianne May wanted kept secret even more than her marriage to you?'

Eric moistened his lips again. 'I don't know what you're talking about. Rianne gave me money because she's my wife. There's nothing more to it than that.'

'I'm wondering why neither of you thought of getting a divorce after you parted.'

Eric shrugged. 'Well, I had left the country and Rianne was too busy probably getting famous to bother—then. You know how it is, I hadn't met anyone I wanted to marry nor probably had Maisie: and so we let things slide. It happens all the time . . .'

Savage looked at him closely without speaking. Then he turned to Roger Petrie who had been listening attentively, a frown between his straight, dark brows. 'I'd rather no further information concerning Rianne May was released to the Press,' the inspector said. 'I daresay that will suit your Publicity Department, too.'

Roger thanked him gravely. 'You can rely on us not to mention what has been said in this room to anyone. But what about Sir Hammond? Should he be informed?'

'I'd be rather surprised if Sir Hammond didn't know already,' was the somewhat cryptic reply as Savage left the room.

Roger Petrie put his shoulders against the door once more and surveyed his team silently.

'Phew!' exclaimed Johnnie Bexhill, mopping his brow without exaggeration. 'I feel wrung out. Fancy Rianne being married all the time to Eric! Sorry, Eric, I didn't mean to sound—'

"Don't bother to apologise,' Eric interrupted. He got up and slouched over to the door. 'I'll clear out and then you can discuss it ad nauseam.'

'I must say you don't seem very concerned about your wife's disappearance,' suggested Greg Oliphant. 'Or is it that you know where she is?'

Eric gave him a look of dislike, but was stopped from replying by Roger, who said quickly: 'Eric, we all know you're in a bit of a spot right now. If there's anything we can do, you can call on us, you know.'

'Good of you,' Eric growled.

Roger put a hand on his arm as he made to open the door. 'There's just one thing. What did Inspector Savage mean about your knowing something more about Rianne?

'How the hell should I know what he meant?' demanded Eric angrily. 'Just leave me alone, damn you! Leave me alone, the lot of you!'

He flung out, slamming the door behind him.

Sue, standing near Roger, said in an undertone: 'I can hardly believe it. Rianne and that disagreeable creature!'

'Oh, Eric's not so bad. You knew nothing about their being married?'

Sue shook her head emphatically. 'Rianne barely mentioned his name. But that's so like her. I won't go so far as to say she had forgotten she once married Eric, but she will have just disregarded the fact.'

'Then the money she paid him could have been for some other reason, as Savage suggested. What was behind his line of questioning, I wonder?'

'I think he's after the cause of Rianne's disappearance still—why and of whom she is afraid.'

'And you haven't been able to suggest anything?'

'The only time I saw Rianne disturbed—other than at the time of the murder, of course—was when I showed her an anonymous letter containing the threat against her life. She gave me the impression that she knew where it came from and that, by ordering me to destroy it, she was trying to banish some . . . some sinister shadow in her life. Does that sound far-fetched?'

Roger did not reply, but his eyes were dark and searching on her face. Presently he said with an unusual abruptness: 'I'd like to have a longer talk, Sue. What about dinner tonight? Can you manage it?'

'Why, yes, I'd like to,' replied Sue, suddenly shy.

'Good! I'll call for you—about seven?'

'I'll be ready,' she returned, her mind flying to her wardrobe. The velour cloth suit or the black two-piece with the little mink tie?

Sue was still undecided about this momentous choice when she dropped into the make-up department later that afternoon to whee-dle a hair-set. It was a relief to forget the tension of the past two days by concentrating solemnly on making herself attractive for a date—especially a date which, she had to admit to herself, she had been anticipating for some time.

'Sure, honey!' Carol agreed, their recent brush apparently forgotten. 'One of the kids can shampoo you, then I'll do the setting.' She gave Sue an up and down look, a queer expression in her eyes. 'Something special, huh?'

Carol's pseudo-American accent was pronounced, as it always was when she was being knowing.

Presently, seated in front of a mirror with her hair dripping darkly on to the towel round her neck, Sue said quickly: 'By the way, Lylah's been on my back about the M.P.S.A.'s treasurership. It looks as if I'm not going to get out of that doubtful honour. I believe you've got some of the books. Do you think you could let me have them some time?'

'Okay!' Carol turned Sue's head from side to side, surveying her reflection with narrowed eyes. 'Something a little more sophisticated, what do you say? You want to make an impression, but in a touch-me-not sort of way.'

She began to roll Sue's hair skilfully. 'You know, if you take my advice you won't—'

'I hope you weren't offended by Lylah's offering me the position,' Sue said. 'I believe you've been assistant treasurer for a couple of years now. She shouldn't have gone over your head like that.'

'Anything my sweet stepsister does is all right in her own opinion. I could tell you quite a few things about the dear girl's methods, too. We'll bring some front hair over your forehead, huh? It'll turn that wide-eyed look of yours into something meaningful.'

'I'm not being prepared for the camera,' objected Sue mildly. 'Oh, all right, then. Yes, it looks pretty good. Thanks, Carol.' She could see herself giving Roger wide-eyed and meaningful looks over a candlelit dinner table, and gave a secret little smile.

'Talking of methods—' began Carol again.

'Perhaps I'd better pick up those books you have,' Sue interrupted, not wanting to disturb her pleasant thoughts of Roger. 'Lylah intends convening a special meeting soon, so I suppose the committee will want some sort of balance sheet.'

'What happened to the one Moya prepared?'

'To tell you the truth, I haven't been through her stuff yet. Do you happen to have a copy?'

'Could do. Moya used to send me screeds of stuff to check. I guess I was never frightfully interested. I'll bring everything round to your flat tonight. Oh, I forgot. You won't be in, will you? Are you sure you should keep this date, Sue? I could tell you—'

'Ted Brown will be at the flat. He has a room next to the garage. And I would like the books as soon as possible.'

Carol was silent. Sue was unable to see her face as she sat with her head tilted forward while Carol pin-curled the lower back hair. 'I wouldn't go out tonight if I were you, Sue,' she said presently. 'Roger's a sweet fellow, but he's got some queer ideas.'

'Who said I was going out with Roger?' asked Sue coldly.

'Johnnie heard you making a date. Look, I mean it, Sue. I wouldn't like to see a friend of mine get in too deep with Roger. There's no future in it—at least not the sort of future you'd like.'

'I'm quite capable of looking after myself, thank you, Carol.'

'Don't be mad at me. If you knew what I knew about this crazy place—'

'What do you know then?'

'Oh, this and that. I'm not prepared to stick my neck out too far. But take it from me—'

'I'm afraid I can't take it from you, Carol. I must have more than vague innuendos to make me change my mind.'

Carol straightened and shrugged. 'Okay, have it your own way.' She fitted a hair net over the immense structure of rollers, slipped in ear shields and wheeled forward a drier. 'But don't blame me if you find yourself in a nasty situation. I've an idea Rianne was—'

But the rest of her words were lost as she switched on the hair-dryer. She dropped the adjusting switch carelessly into Sue's lap and left her.

Sue didn't see Carol again. One of the other girls was sent over to comb her hair.

Sue tried the effect of the new hair-style and the ensemble with the mink tie on Ted Brown before Roger called for her that evening. He was doing something under the bonnet of the Mercedes as she came down the stairs from the flat. The tap-tap of her high heels made him look up. At first he looked surprised at her appearance and then slowly his eyes lit up admiringly. 'You look stunning!' he observed simply. 'Can I give you a lift anywhere?'

'Thank you for the compliment!' Sue dropped a little mock curt-sy. 'And the offer. But I'm being called for. I just wanted to tell you Carol Frazer might drop in a parcel for me later.'

'Any message?'

Sue saw a low convertible coming round the corner. 'Yes, thank her for doing my hair, will you? Good night, Ted!

'Good night,' he echoed slowly, leaning over the bonnet to watch her departure.

Roger's eyes rested on her at dinner with restrained appreciation. He had chosen a quiet restaurant, but one that was evidently a popu-lar rendezvous with television people. There were smiles and waves from various other diners, whom Sue only half-recognised without their camera make-up. She was proud of Roger's indifference to the curious glances directed at her. After all, he belonged to that stra-tum of society which provided material for the TV magazine gossip columnists.

They talked only briefly of Rianne and the trouble surrounding her. Sue was reluctant to let it intrude on the wonderful evening, so presently Roger began to talk of his work and his plans for the future.

She listened happily, watching him unconsciously with the wide-eyed look Carol had mentioned.

'I do hope I'm not boring you,' he broke off to say, now and then.

'No, no! Please go on. You make television sound so absorbing and thrilling. I hadn't stopped to realise how, as a medium, it can be used for better things than a view of Rianne's neckline.' She felt quite daring saying this but he did not laugh, which somehow disappointed her.

He pushed aside his coffee cup and leant closer to her, his eyes glowing. 'Sue, it's great to talk to someone who has so much understanding and intelligence. I thought, when I first saw you, that you would be a girl with ideals as well as ideas.'

Sue's heartbeat quickened and the warm colour flooded her cheeks. But all she could find to say was: 'I'm quite ordinary, really.'

He picked up her hand and held it between both his. 'You mustn't say that. If you are, then it's only because you haven't had a chance yet. There's something deep inside you that is calling out for fulfilment. You're the sort of person this poor, sick world needs. It's people like you who can help put television on the right lines. The poor, duped public think they know what they want, but actually it's only people like you and me, who are prepared to serve others, who know what is good for them.'

Roger spoke so intently that Sue gave a nervous laugh. 'I was told you had some . . . some unusual ideas.'

'Is that what you think they are?'

'No, indeed,' she returned quickly, not wishing to hurt his feelings.

He released her hand and signalled to the waiter for the bill. 'Will you come to a party some people I know are giving? You'll enjoy it, I think.'

Glad that their date was not ending with dinner, Sue said: 'I'm sure I will.'

But she was not quite so certain when they arrived at an impressive mansion in a fashionable suburb. 'Who's giving this party?' she asked, surveying the immense facade of the house and then turning to follow with her eye the sweep of the driveway vanishing through the spacious grounds.

Roger told her the name of her hostess. 'A charming woman—not clever, but very dedicated.'

'What is she dedicated to?' asked Sue, laughing. 'Giving parties?'

'It's her way of helping a cause.'

'What cause?' asked Sue, bewildered, allowing Roger to guide her through the open front door.

At once they were caught up in a crowd of people, some distinguished-looking and well-dressed. It was a muted sort of party, with the guests drinking leisurely and talking quietly. A young man with a lock of dark hair falling over his brow was playing the grand piano in an unobtrusive fashion. There seemed to be very little party spirit and, what struck Sue as odd, very little laughter.

'How odd!' she repeated to herself, and immediately was reminded of Mother Paul, who so often used the word. Then for some reason—whether it was thinking of the nun or the unnatural restraint of the gathering—she began to feel uneasy.

Roger kept drawing her from group to group, introducing her to people with vaguely familiar names. She identified a university professor, an industrial leader and a couple of politicians. They were all very friendly.

'Enjoying yourself?' asked Roger, putting a drink into her hand.

'Yes, of course, but—'

'There's Editha! Come and meet her.'

Their hostess was dyed, curled, jewelled and gushing. Her restless, made-up eyes darted from Sue to Roger, to the people about her, as though she didn't know where they all came from—which, as Sue was to discover, was true. 'All these frantically clever people! Aren't they wonderful? Too marvellous to be able to do one's little bit alongside them. Ah, this poor, sick world! Has this sweet child signed the visitor's book yet, Roger? Take her into the den. There's the senator waving—I must go!'

Poor, sick world! That was the second time this evening Sue had heard that phrase. She pulled away from Roger's guiding hand. 'What is all this about?' she demanded, half-amused, half-apprehensive. 'Where are you taking me now?'

'To sign the book. You don't mind, do you?'

'Why should I sign it?' asked Sue dubiously. 'I'm not that important, and I don't want to let myself in for anything without knowing what it's all about. If you'd only explain what—'

'Just as soon as I can. You know you can trust me, don't you, Sue?' Roger's grave eyes looked deeply into hers.

'Yes, of course I trust you,' she replied, but her uneasiness was growing and she felt out of place in this big, handsome house with its dithery, superficial hostess and the strange assortment of guests.

Roger said: 'Good evening, sir' to a tall man with a head of grey curling hair and a moustache, who looked and spoke like a mid-European. Sue couldn't remember his unpronounceable name. He began asking her questions about Rianne, saying he was sorry that he hadn't met her in his country yet—that Sue must see to it that she came the next time.

Sue looked at Roger and then at the mid-European, then at the rest of the room in much the same way as Editha had done. Her brain was in a whirl and she felt a strong impulse to run. Faces seemed to be staring at her and closing in.

Then, suddenly, just as in a nightmare when some familiar person appears incongruously, she saw the tall figure of Ted Brown. Ted—here? For a moment Sue gasped in surprise. And even he was looking different. His face was not wearing its customary easy-going grin: instead, it was set in hard lines and even his loping walk had become purposeful striding.

He came straight to where Sue was standing with Roger and the mid-European and stood silently surveying them all. Embarrassed, because both Roger and his companion had stopped their conversation and were looking at her in amazement, Sue made an attempt at introducing Roger but Ted ignored both men and said loudly and sharply: 'Your headache seems to have vanished remarkably quickly. If you are able to come here, then you were fit enough to stand by our appointment. I would not mind so much for myself, but my friends had planned dinner for us . . . if we hurry, we can make it.'

Sue could hardly believe her own ears. It was all exactly like a nightmare, she told herself again, when even the mildest people do the wildest things. But there was no doubt about the solidity of Ted's presence—and you could almost hear the heavy silence in the room.

'But, Ted,' she stammered nervously, wishing she could sink through the floor. 'What do you . . . I mean . . .'

'Look here, Brown,' Roger said sternly. 'This is a private party and you've no business here at all. In fact, I've yet to discover how the devil you got in here—but if you are bent on picking a quarrel, then I suggest you postpone it until tomorrow. I should be glad if you would leave now.'

For answer, Ted took Sue's arm in a firm grasp and began to draw her away. She felt helpless in the face of such surprising behaviour and looked appealingly at Roger who was now glowering with rage. Fearing more trouble, Sue said quickly: 'I'm sorry about all this, Roger, but I really think I'd better slip out now. Make my apologies to everyone when we've gone—please.'

The guests made way for them and Sue heard several titters as she passed. It was an agonising few moments but, all the same, she felt relieved to be away from that strangely disturbing gathering.

The Mercedes was standing in the middle of the drive. Ted pushed her gently into it and ran round to the other side.

'Oh, Ted, I was never so glad to see anyone in my life!' Sue exclaimed as the engine throbbed under his foot. She glanced furtively over her shoulder as they tore through the gates. 'There was something wrong, terribly wrong! Roger—how did you know?'

'Don't try and talk now. Just relax,' Ted suggested gently.

'And it was going to be such a lovely night!' Sue said tremulously. To her horror, great tears welled into her eyes and she gulped like a child, feverishly searching for her handkerchief.

Ted speeded the car round a couple of corners. In a quiet, dark street he pulled up with a jerk and, turning, put his arm about her and drew her close.

Sue pressed her face into his shoulder and sobbed unrestrainedly. 'I'm a fool—a fool!' she kept saying, while Ted made inarticulate but soothing sounds. Presently she lifted her head and blew her nose. 'I'm all right now,' she said shyly. 'Thanks for the loan of the shoulder. Let's go home now.'

Ted removed himself reluctantly and re-started the car. They were both silent for several minutes. Then Sue, who had been slowly collecting her wits, asked: 'How did you know where I was?'

He gave an embarrassed grunt. 'I followed you.'

'Followed me? Why?' She bent forward, trying to look into his face. Ted was behaving entirely out of character. He seemed so serious and yet so gentle that she felt vaguely disturbed all over again.

'Why did you follow me, Ted?' she persisted.

'Perhaps I was jealous,' he said. He was smiling now, but his eyes were as inscrutable as ever as he turned to her.

And suddenly Sue was annoyed: annoyed at the curious twist in her heart which his words had caused, annoyed at his impish grin, his refusal to be the Ted who had become so familiar to her and whom she had often despised. 'What right have you to be jealous?' she managed to blurt out. 'And what right have you to come snooping after me? You made me look a fool.' Gone was the gratitude she had felt towards him for taking her from a place which had seemed sinister to her.

Ted gave a short laugh, whether of amusement or bitterness, she couldn't make out. 'Much better for you to look a fool than get involved with something you know nothing about—although what induced you to go with a softie like Petrie I'll never know. I credited you with more sense than that, I must say.'

Remembering the feelings Roger Petrie had always aroused in her made Sue feel ashamed now, but she wasn't going to let Ted know that. Instead, she said haughtily: 'I don't know what you mean, and I would remind you that it is none of your business what I do.'

He ignored the remark, looking steadfastly at the road. 'You're right there, Sue,' he said at last. 'But I am not going to apologise for my behaviour—you're far too nice a girl to become involved with that kind of mob. They might call themselves the Servants of Peace or any other fancy title and talk a lot of bull about curing the poor, sick world, but it's not servants they aim to be. It's masters, dictators . . . now do you see what I mean? And you can thank your lucky stars they haven't got you properly shackled by now.'

'You mean they're some kind of political movement—out for power? Like Hitler? Oh, Ted, I did wonder once or twice. And Roger Petrie? You mean he deliberately tried to—' She broke off, her mind whirling once more. 'Oh, no,' she said brokenly.

She remembered a discussion about the destructive force of power;

how power-ridden men always used the Press to further their ambition and, now that television was so popular, it occurred to her that you could feed people subtly with propaganda, even through such performers as Rianne . . . that was why the leaders of such groups wanted to get hold of actors, authors, politicians, knowing that the ordinary man in the street could swallow doctrines without even realising. It was horrible. And that Roger Petrie should just have been using her . . . because Rianne had tried to withdraw, he had thought that Sue as her secretary could . . . no, no! It was too dreadful to contemplate, too humiliating when she had been dreaming dreams, feeding her hopes on such falseness.

And it had been Ted—Ted Brown—who had rescued her! It was no good: the tears began to fall again and she turned abruptly to look out of the window, blinded though she was, so that Ted should not notice.

'Don't let it upset you,' said Ted, his voice oddly authoritative yet kind. 'He's not worth it, Sue.'

'But how do you know all this?' she asked in a small voice. 'Did Inspector Savage tell you? Does he know about Roger and that . . . that house back there?'

'He did mention it, yes,' admitted Ted.

'In connection with Rianne? There was a guest there tonight actually, a foreigner who seemed to be the centre of the party. I can't remember his name, but he was asking me about Rianne. I didn't care for the way he spoke about her, as though . . . what did you call it? Shackled, that's it—as though she were shackled. Those dates Rianne broke with Roger . . . Ted, he could have been trying to get her to that house . . .'

Sue waited for Ted to comment, but he gave a non-committal grunt.

'Are you sure the inspector knows about this organisation—these Servants of Peace? Suppose . . . suppose Rianne knew too much about them and was intending to go to the police with her information. Suppose they threatened her—that note—or even kidnapped her!' Her thoughts were running riot now, making her strangely nervous. Let's get home quickly, Ted. I'm going to ring the inspector and tell him about tonight.'

But the telephone was already ringing when they got to the flat. Sue hurried over to it and then stopped, wondering if it might be Roger Petrie and what she could possibly say to him now that she knew what his intentions had been. She glanced over her shoulder at Ted as though to gain reassurance from his stolid presence and then lifted the receiver.

'Sue?' asked a female voice at once. 'This is Janet. I've been trying to get you for ages. Can you come at once?

'Janet?'

Janet Gordon. Look, there's no time to waste. We've got Carol here. She's in a pretty bad way and she's asking for you. Better get over here just as soon as you can.'

'Over where?' Sue felt as though the nightmare was swamping her once more.

'What's the matter with you, Sue?' said the voice sharply. 'You know me—Dr Janet Gordon! We met at the notorious Maryhill reunion. Listen closely and I'll tell you how to get to the hospital from your place. Hurry! Carol hasn't got much time left, poor kid!'

9

Carol was dead by the time Sue and Ted arrived at the hospital. She had been struck by a car not far from Rianne's flat. The driver had not stopped.

Janet Gordon was waiting in the foyer to tell them the news. She was brisk and matter-of-fact, but her face was nearly as white as the resident's coat she wore. 'Carol was brought into Casualty,' she explained, glancing indifferently at Ted. 'They found a letter from Maryhill in her bag when they were looking for identification. Someone remembered I went to school there and they called me down. I think she knew me. She wanted me to send for you, Sue. Have you any idea why?'

'Please, Janet, not now!' Sue said brokenly. 'I can't think.'

'Pull yourself together!' Dr Gordon said but her voice was kind. 'The police are here and they want to ask questions.'

'The police?' echoed Sue stupidly.

'They came with the ambulance. Then that Inspector character arrived a short time ago. You know, the one who came to Maryhill the day Moya was murdered. Mother Paul's pal. I told him you were on your way.'

'But why is he here? Wasn't it an accident?' The flicker of fear that seemed to have been with Sue for days now flared up again, threatening to overwhelm her.

Janet shrugged. 'Don't ask me, ask him. My opinion is the coincidence of a hit and run driver and a victim closely associated with his case was too much for him. This is the way!'

She strode ahead in her large, sensible shoes, her stethoscope protruding from one pocket.

Inspector Savage was standing at a table in one of the waiting-rooms. He was going through Carol's belongings, a handbag and a briefcase she had been carrying. There was a smear of blood on the handbag. A couple of younger, uniformed policemen were with him. He looked up when Sue and Ted came in and nodded briefly. Then, without preamble, he said: 'Dr Gordon says Miss Frazer kept calling for you, Miss Berry. Can you tell me why?'

Ted prompted Sue gently. 'You did say she might call at the flat this evening, Sue.'

'Oh, yes, of course. How stupid of me to forget!' She passed a hand across her forehead in a dazed gesture. 'Carol was bringing me some papers connected with Maryhill, Inspector. After Moya Curran was . . . after she died, Lylah Willis asked me to be treasurer.'

'Would these be the papers you are referring to?' Savage pushed the briefcase across to her. She fingered its contents gingerly and then nodded.

'If she were on her way to see you,' continued Savage thoughtfully, 'then that could account for her having your name in mind. Or have you some other suggestion, Miss Berry?'

'There is another possibility,' Sue replied quietly. 'We had a slight disagreement in the afternoon about a date I had this evening. I didn't know where I was going to be taken, but I imagine Carol suspected. I realise now that she was sincerely trying to warn me.'

'And where were you taken, Miss Berry?'

'To the home of a woman called Editha. I didn't catch her surname. She was entertaining an organisation called the Servants of Peace. Ted says you know about them.'

Savage gave Ted a quick glance. 'Yes, that is so. They are affiliated with a group in England and the United States.'

'Did you know Rianne was mixed up with them in some way?'

'Yes, we've known that for quite some time. But unfortunately we haven't been able to tie up Miss May's disappearance with them. Although the group is suspect, so far there has been nothing criminal about their activities. Like all these groups, the real villains remain hidden in the background, well screened. Perhaps Miss Frazer may have been able to identify one of them. She had the rather dangerous habit of letting it appear that she knew something sinister about other people.'

Janet spoke for the first time: 'Yes, Carol was like that. But I sometimes wondered whether she hadn't more hunches than real facts.'

'You speak from experience, Dr Gordon?'

Janet met his look squarely. 'Of her hunches, yes! But not of any facts she possessed.'

Savage picked up a slip of paper from the table and unfolded it. 'Something to do with this? A prescription written by you on the evening of the day of Miss Curran's murder?'

Janet took the paper. 'A prescription for a mild sedative which was made up in the dispensary of this hospital. She wanted something to calm her nerves after the shock of Moya's death. Actually she could have purchased something just as effective from any chemist.'

'But instead she used it as an excuse to come and see you. Is that right?'

Janet's teeth gleamed briefly. 'Quite right! I won't waste your time. Even if Carol were deliberately killed tonight, I have a watertight alibi. I've been in view of hospital staff or patients since four o'clock this afternoon.'

'Why did Miss Frazer use such a flimsy pretext in order to see you, Doctor?'

Janet replied without hesitation. 'She wanted to find out what Rianne was hinting about me at the tea-table that ghastly Reunion Day. You remember, Sue? I don't blame Rianne for wanting to get her own back. I remember I gave her a hell of a time at school. But it really shook me that she was referring to a rather unsavoury peccadillo of mine. I hoped she was only bluffing. After all, it happened years ago and we were only youngsters, but that sort of thing could still be pretty damaging to the career of a woman doctor.

'Do you wish me to be more explicit, Inspector? Or may I spare young Sue's blushes? And perhaps one or two of my own,' she added with a touch of bitterness.

'Did Carol succeed in trapping you into some sort of admission?'

'I am not easily trapped,' retorted Janet. 'I made it quite clear to Carol that I was intending to have it out with Rianne with a suit for slander if need be. She wasn't hard to scare.'

'Who wasn't?' asked Savage casually.

'Young Carol. Rianne wasn't in when I—' Janet broke off, and Savage looked at her without speaking. 'Clever!' she nodded in approval. '*You* certainly trapped me, though.'

'Carol knew Rianne had disappeared before the news was released. I was wondering how she knew. That could only mean, Doctor, that you were in Miss May's flat while I was there with Miss Berry and Sir Hammond Willis.'

'Right again!' agreed Janet. 'After you allowed us to leave Maryhill, I went straight to Rianne's place. She wasn't in, but as the door was open, I knew she couldn't be far away. When that husband of Lylah's turned up, I nipped into the kitchen. Then the rest of you arrived and . . . well, somehow I just stayed to hear what was going on. That's all.'

'You have been wonderfully frank, Dr Gordon,' observed Savage dryly.

'I have nothing to hide,' she retorted.

'Nor even Rianne May?' asked Savage sternly.

'I won't dissemble by asking what you mean,' she answered coolly. 'You're wondering if I have Rianne hidden somewhere. Well, I haven't. She neither appealed to me to hide her, not did I lure her away. She was definitely not at the flat when I arrived. And, later, when young Carol hinted that she intended asking Rianne about the trouble between us, I told her not to waste her time as I had it on good authority that she had vamoosed.'

'Since you are laying cards on the table with such vigour,' said Savage genially, 'perhaps you will answer this question. Was your fear of what Rianne May could disclose about your, er, schoolgirl past strong enough to make you want to silence her?'

Janet grinned again, but she was still rather white. 'I've had to battle quite a bit in my career, Inspector, but I don't carry cyanide everywhere I go as a precaution against enemies. Not that I couldn't have got hold of the stuff, as I told Mother Paul on the telephone one day. Curiously enough, she was asking me much the same questions as you—but more tactfully phrased, if you don't mind my saying so. But I assure you that if I had, on the spur of the moment, decided to get rid of Rianne I wouldn't have made a botch of it and murdered someone else instead.'

'No, I don't think you would have, Doctor,' agreed Savage suavely. 'And I'm sure Mother Paul wouldn't think so, either.'

Janet turned her head. 'Sue, have you seen her lately? How is the poor old dear? She started spouting the strangest rubbish—something about your telling her television studios are not as big and elaborate as they seem on camera.'

'I saw her the evening after the reunion. She was all right then. She'd just knocked an escaped lunatic unconscious,' added Sue with a tired smile.

Janet made an attempt to laugh. 'Yes, I heard about that.' Through the glass partitions of the waiting-room she saw a nurse approaching. 'Do you want me any more, Inspector? I am supposed to be on duty.'

The nurse put her head in. She cast a curious glance at the policemen. 'Doctor Gordon, there are some people in the foyer by the name of Willis. And another man who says he's the girl's fiancé.'

'I sent for Lylah, too,' explained Janet. 'After all, she is Carol's stepsister.'

Savage spoke to the two policemen: 'I'll finish up here for you. On your way out, ask Sir Hammond and Lady Willis to come here. And Mr Bexhill, too.'

'I think I'll stick around for a while,' Janet remarked. 'This could be interesting. Tell them to call on the intercom, if I'm wanted, will you, Sister?'

Savage repacked Carol's handbag and the briefcase. He handed the latter to Sue. 'I gather you will want to have this. It seems to hold nothing but accounts.'

Janet watched the approach of the Willises. 'Come on in, Lylah,' she invited calmly, looking the two men over as if they were prospective patients. 'I haven't met your husband before, or this other gentleman. I am Doctor Gordon. But I believe you all know Inspector Savage.'

'What on earth is he doing here?' demanded Lylah, giving Savage the barest nod. 'And Sue Berry! What's all this about Carol's having an accident, Janet?'

Janet, regarding her closely, announced bluntly: 'Carol is dead, Lylah. I'm sorry,' she added quickly to Johnnie Bexhill, who let out a horrified gasp. 'Here, sit down. I shouldn't have told you so abruptly.

Forgive me. I forgot about your being engaged to Carol.'

Sue moved towards Johnnie and put a hand on his shoulder. He stared at her, dazed and uncomprehending. 'She's dead? Carol? No! No!'

'Yes, Johnnie,' Sue said gently. 'A hit and run driver.' He gave a groan and buried his face in his hands. His shoulders shook. Janet said quietly to Ted: 'Slip out and find that sister. Tell her we have someone all to pieces in here. She'll know what to bring.'

'Steady, Johnnie!' said Sir Hammond, gripping the young man's shoulder. He was looking pale and shaken himself. 'This is appalling news, Inspector. Poor little Carol! How did it happen?'

'Miss Frazer was on her way to Miss Berry's flat, I understand. She was struck by a car while crossing the road. We've got men out trying to locate the driver. Unfortunately, it was a back street and there were no witnesses.'

'You mean there's not much chance of finding this . . . this murderer?'

The inspector's brows shot up, but before he could speak, Lylah said haughtily: 'You mustn't take any notice of my husband, Inspector. He is not quite himself. He was very fond of Carol, like an elder brother to her. The shock has been terrible for both of us. These hit and run drivers are abominable. They shouldn't be allowed to get away with easy sentences, even if it is an accident.

'And if it isn't an accident, Lady Willis?'

'I don't follow you,' she retorted sharply. 'Carol was always a foolhardy girl. She was nearly involved in an accident before. I remember her saying so at the reunion.

'My dear!' Sir Hammond said wearily. 'Nothing you can say will alter the fact that Inspector Savage had very good reasons for being here. Suppose we listen to what he has to say.'

'Really, Hammond!' Lylah was definitely affronted.

'Yes, try to keep quiet, Lylah,' said Janet. 'You carried on in much the same way when Moya was killed. You're frightened but no one blames you for that!'

Lylah's face quivered with anger. Ignoring Janet with an effort, she addressed Savage: 'Well, what do you want to say?'

'Just this, Lady Willis! Whether your stepsister's death was an accident or not, I cannot ignore the fact that she has been implicated all along in the case I am investigating. Until the circumstances of her death are clarified, I must suspect the possibility of her having been deliberately run down.'

'But why should anyone want to kill Carol?' persisted Lady Willis in her dogged fashion.

'That's what I must make enquiries about. Now suppose you tell me where you were this evening.'

'How dare you! exclaimed Lylah furiously. 'I refuse to answer your impertinent question!'

Johnnie Bexhill, who had revived somewhat after drinking the contents of a medicine glass that Ted had quietly brought back to him, lurched unsteadily to his feet.

'You hated Carol, Lady Willis. She told me. You hated her because—' He broke off and glanced at Sir Hammond. The glance developed into a brooding stare.

'Steady, Johnnie!' said Sir Hammond again. But he sounded uneasy.

'Very well, I'll tell you, Inspector,' said Lylah in a loud voice. 'I was very fond of my stepsister and always tried to do my duty by her. Both my husband and I tried, even though she was wayward and ungrateful. Why it should concern you, I can't imagine, but I was at home all the evening preparing a speech I am making at a hospital board meeting tomorrow.'

'Thank you, Lady Willis!' Savage made a note in his book. 'And was Sir Hammond at home, too?'

'No, I was at my club, Inspector. I think there will be people who can vouch for that. But my wife's friend, Mrs Hurley, spent the evening with her. I always seem to have a long-standing engagement to dine at my club whenever Eunice comes,' he added suavely.

'Was there anyone in the house besides Mrs Hurley and yourself, Lady Willis?'

Lylah was sitting bolt upright, staring at her husband. 'No, no one else.'

'When did you last see Miss Frazer?'

'I haven't seen Carol since that day of the reunion at Maryhill. I spoke to her on the telephone a couple of times.'

'What about?'

Lylah transferred her gaze to Savage's face, her eyes growing cold and haughty. 'To tell her Miss Berry was appointed treasurer and to pass over to her any books or accounts she might have.'

'Did you speak about anything else?'

'I don't remember exactly. I suppose we discussed Rianne and Moya.'

'What was the gist of that discussion, Lady Willis?'

'About who was going to Moya's funeral and what flowers the committee would send.'

'Was that the extent of the discussion, or did you and Miss Frazer perhaps speculate what might have happened to Rianne? And who would have wanted to murder her?'

'I don't remember,' repeated Lylah, mulishly.

'But you said just now that you might have discussed Rianne as well as Moya, Lady Willis. You've told us what was said about Miss Curran. Now I would like you to tell me about Miss May.'

'I wasn't listening closely.'

'You mean Carol was talking about Rianne? What did she say?'

'Hammond, isn't there any way you can stop this man from pestering me?'

'His questions are reasonable enough, my dear. But if you like, I can get hold of a lawyer.'

'Certainly not! There is no need for that, surely!' snapped Lady Willis ungratefully. 'Carol said something about there being more to the case than met the eye, Inspector. She hinted at knowing something of Rianne's past life. As if anyone couldn't guess that that woman had an unsavoury past! Do you wonder I didn't pay much attention!'

'Were your relations with Miss Frazer friendly? Was there ever any quarrel between you?'

'I was always disposed to being friendly,' replied Lylah grandly, but, as I told you before, Carol showed no signs of gratitude for all I . . . we had done for her. And what might that vulgar sound mean, Janet?'

'Lylah, you're a fool! Everyone knows—including the astute inspector—that you and Carol loathed each other. You heard what her young man said only a few moments ago.'

'Yes, you hated her—Carol told me,' repeated Johnnie dully. 'And she despised you, too. She used to laugh about you. And you!' he told Sir Hammond viciously. He shook his head as though to clear it. 'But I was never quite sure whether she really meant what she said. She might have been trying to fob me off.'

'Fob you off what, Mr Bexhill?' asked Savage quietly.

'About the . . . the relationship between her and Sir Hammond. He sent her on that trip, you know. And I guess he was paying the rent for the flat. Carol never would admit it outright. She was like that. You never knew how much she meant or what she was really thinking. She was the kind of girl who'd always keep you in suspense. I didn't even like to ask her when we'd get married. I tried once and she . . . she . . . I couldn't have borne it if she'd thrown me over. And now she's gone! Do you know, in a way, it's a relief? She doesn't belong to anyone now.'

'Johnnie, hush!' said Sue urgently. 'You don't know what you're saying.'

'That's all right, Miss Berry,' the inspector said. 'I'm prepared to make allowances for the awful shock he must have sustained. Tell me, Johnnie, when did you last see Carol?'

'This evening,' he replied vacantly. 'After he'd gone.'

'Who? Sir Hammond?'

'Yes,' Sir Hammond answered quickly. 'I called on Carol on the way to the club. There was nothing unusual in that. I dropped in now and then to see how she was—in an elder-brotherly way, of course,' he added with an ironic glance at his wife.

'And how did you find Miss Frazer, Sir Hammond?'

He drew his brows together. 'She was a little distrait, I thought. She'd been speaking to someone on the telephone when I arrived. As a matter of fact, I was going to tell you about it. It could have some significance. I heard her say something about discussing the matter further, but that in her mind there was no doubt and she thought the police ought to know.'

'Did you ask her about this call and what she meant?'

'Yes, I did, because she seemed rather startled to see me. I asked her what it was she thought the police ought to know, but she dodged the question. Carol rather enjoyed being enigmatic, you know. She said—really, it's rather difficult to recall how she put it—something about the matter not having anything to do with the case or with me. Then she looked at me rather queerly and added that perhaps it did have something to do with the case and could involve me, after all. I found her attitude somewhat irritating, so I left.'

Savage seemed to digest that information carefully for a moment, then he turned to Johnnie: 'You saw Sir Hammond leave?'

'I drew up just as his car moved off.'

'And how did you find Miss Frazer?'

'Something like Sir Hammond said. But then,' said Johnnie humbly, 'she was always a bit off-hand with me. Always acting as though she were thinking of something else. I couldn't get near her. I tried different ways, told her bits of gossip from the studio because I knew she liked to know what was going on. She liked to laugh about people. She was laughing about Sue Berry as she was packing up that briefcase she's got now. I asked Carol if Sue had gone out this evening, after all. She'd told me she was going to try to stop her. Poor Sue!" she said. "She's going to be in more trouble than she knows how to handle. It'll be interesting to see how soon she'll be a wake-up." '

Sue felt her face burn as all eyes turned on her. She was thankful the inspector already knew about the earlier events of the evening.

'Whatever can Carol have meant?' demanded Lylah, eyeing Sue accusingly. I don't like to hear that you are in trouble, Suzanne.'

'You can save your officious sympathy, Lylah,' suggested Janet dryly. 'You're in enough trouble of your own.'

'Indeed? I am not aware of being implicated in any way.'

Sir Hammond surveyed his wife with an admiration tinged with mockery. 'Your powers of self-deception are quite remarkable, my dear. Well, Inspector? What now?'

'Nothing more for the moment,' replied Savage mildly.

10

Carol Frazer's death gave fresh impetus to the Rianne May news story. Sue was surprised that Savage had released the information so freely. He had even allowed himself to be quoted as declaring there to be a definite link between the two deaths and the continued hidden whereabouts of the famous television star. Evidently, with the failure to find the hit and run driver, he was prepared to throw caution to the winds and openly affirm his suspicions as to the nature of Carol's death.

Sue read the newspapers as she toyed with a combined breakfast and lunch the following day. She had called Ted on the extension to his room earlier to say she intended staying at home all day, and to inform the studio when he went there to report. Then she had gone back to bed, to lie as tensed and sleepless as she had all night. The telephone rang several times and she listened to its ringing with miserable disinterest.

It was after midday when she made the effort to rouse herself from her lethargy. The telephone rang again as she was passing it on her way to the bathroom, and she picked it up automatically.

'Sue?' asked a gentle, lilting voice. 'How are you, dear child? So shocking about Carol Frazer! Janet has been giving me details and, of course, it's in the papers, too. Poor Mr Savage—he must be quite exasperated. Things have really gone too far. We must stop this wicked person at once, don't you agree, Sue?'

'Yes, Mother Paul,' said Sue wearily.

'You sound worn out, child. That nice Mr Brown said you were staying at home to rest. I tried to get you at the studio first and they put me on to him. Just like a faithful watch-dog, so I asked him to come, too.'

'Come where, Mother Paul?'

'Why here to Maryhill, dear! I can't be running round outside my convent. Although I must say there have been times recently when I would have liked to. But it's quite amazing how much investigating one can do on the telephone. Mind you, I'm not absolutely certain I'm correct. There's a small piece missing, but I'm sure if we can all discuss the case together, we'll soon find it. Did I tell you there was a message from Mr Savage that he would be coming, too?'

Sue's hand gripped the receiver hard. 'Mother Paul!' she exclaimed incredulously. 'Are you suggesting that you know who murdered Moya and Carol and why Rianne has vanished?'

The nun's voice held a note of humility: 'Yes, dear. It does sound presumptuous, I know. I only wish I had the missing small piece. But I daresay you might be able to help there. Shall we say seven this evening then? And now I must go. My bell is ringing.'

'No, Mother Paul, wait! You can't possibly . . . Does Mr Savage? . . . Mother Paul!' But the nun had hung up.

Slowly Sue replaced the receiver, remembering what Janet had said about the nun the night before. It really did seem that Mother Paul was slightly unhinged. Then she thought of the earlier telephone calls and wondered who had been trying to contact her. Roger Petrie, perhaps, after that last ghastly meeting? She found herself sinking into an apathy of misery again and, but for the possibility of meeting Roger, almost wished she had gone to the studio after all.

What you want, my girl, is some work to do! she told herself severely.

But there was little she could find to do in the flat after she had eaten and washed up the dishes. Now and then she found herself standing aimlessly in the middle of the room, thinking of the sequence of events that had brought her to this moment. Rianne seemed a far-away stranger now, almost as though she had never existed. Only the chaos she had left behind her was real. The chances of Mother Paul actually knowing something that might enable the inspector to sort out the chaos seemed remote.

How could the nun know about Rianne's secret marriage to Eric

Watts and the possibility of blackmailing her, for example? Or Roger's association with a subversive political movement and his attempts to implicate both Rianne and herself? She might be aware of the unhappy machinations of the Willis family because of their daughter Sandra being a boarder at Maryhill, but she couldn't possibly know about Johnnie Bexhill's blind devotion to Carol or the so-called affair Greg Oliphant had had with Rianne.

Carol's briefcase containing the Maryhill Past Students' Association papers caught her eye as it lay on the couch where she had dropped it uncaringly the previous night. Now she went over to it and, after a moment's irresolution, began to look for the other books that Mother Paul had given her belonging to Moya. Presently she had them all spread out on her desk, in a desperate attempt to clear her mind for a moment of Rianne and the tragedy which followed her.

It took quite some time to sort out the various statements and accounts. Moya had been an earnest treasurer but a poor accountant, with a system all her own. She had had the habit of lumping expenditure together under such a vague heading as Miscellaneous Expenses. After a fruitless search for a balance sheet, Sue set about preparing one of her own, covering sheet after sheet of her scribbling block with figures.

The winter afternoon closed in as she worked and she got up to switch on the lights. The balance sheet was causing her despair—it just wouldn't balance. Once more she went laboriously through every item in the ledgers and cash books and finally checked the cheque butts. There were two trust funds—one for a student scholarship, the other to provide amenities for the school. It seemed to Sue that neither fund had been accurately accounted for. The bank statements showed a far lower amount than those entered in the books. After a lot more checking, she found the discrepancies and sat back to ponder on them.

Presently she picked up a Maryhill letterhead and, pulling the telephone towards her, dialled Lylah Willis's number. She allowed it to ring for quite some time and then replaced the receiver with an exclamation of impatience. She had reached a stage where it was impossible to continue without consulting some executive member of the Association.

The front doorbell chimed and Sue's mind flashed back to the present. Her hands gripped the edge of her desk tensely and she held her breath. It rang again and she told herself that she was behaving foolishly. Reluctantly she got up and went to the door. After a third ring she forced herself to open it.

'Why, hello!' she said, relief and surprise mingled in her voice. 'Come on in!'

At Maryhill, Mother Paul was called to the phone just as the chapel bell was ringing for Vespers.

'It's Sue, Mother Paul!'

'Sue? Is anything wrong?' the girl sounded gay and alert, very different from the tired girl the nun had spoken to earlier. There was an excitement about the voice which made Mother Paul feel strangely uneasy.

'Everything's just fine! But I may be a bit late for your meeting tonight. Please tell Inspector Savage to wait. I've a surprise for him.'

'Have you, dear?' asked the nun doubtfully. 'What sort of surprise?'

'I think I know where Rianne is. There's more than gold in them thar hills! I hope to bring her to Maryhill. Mother Paul, isn't it marvellous? I can hardly believe it myself! And now I must go,' she added, in gentle parody. 'I've got someone waiting in a car.'

'No, Sue, wait! You must tell me —' But a click in Mother Paul's ear announced that the girl had cut off. 'Oh, the naughty, foolish child! If only she'd told me where she is going! What shall I do now?'

'Are you all right, Reverend Mother?' asked a young nun timidly. The telephone was situated in an ante-room near the chapel and the community was filing through for Vespers.

Mother Paul looked into the sweet, anxious face. 'Sister, who is the best saint for a really desperate emergency?'

The young nun replied earnestly: 'What about St. Thalburga, Mother? After all, she did save us the other night.'

'Then she might consider she's done enough. Go on in, Sister, and try every saint in the calendar. Oh, dear, I wish one could apply for supernatural help the way one can call the police,' she murmured, as she dialled with a none too steady finger. 'I want Inspector Robert Savage of the C.I.B. at once, please!'

'Reverend Mother, we are waiting for you,' whispered another nun.

'Yes, yes, I'm coming. Tell Mother Eugene to commence. Mr Savage? What? Oh, no! Please try and locate him. I'll hold on!'

Presently a peal sounded from the organ loft above her head followed by the clear, passionless voices of her sisters-in-religion chanting the opening of Vespers.

'Deus in adjutorium meum intende,' she sang softly and reverently, only to break off when the voice came back to say that Inspector Savage had left the building but could be located later at Maryhill Girls' School.

With a great fear in her heart, Mother Paul tried two other numbers, but at neither could she get in touch with the person she wanted. There was nothing she could do now but wait. Her nuns were too well disciplined even to glance in her direction as she glided to her prie-dieu. Mother Paul adjusted her horn-rimmed spectacles on her short soft nose, picked up her volume of the Divine Office and, with a serenity she was far from feeling, raised her voice with the others.

She had calculated that it would be at least an hour or even more before the inspector arrived. But, to her relief, the doorbell rang just as they were leaving the chapel. 'I'll go, Sister,' she said, sweeping ahead of the lay nun whose task it was to be portress.

She flung the door wide, but it was not Savage who stood on the step but Ted Brown. He stepped in quickly, saying in a strange, clipped voice: 'Where is Sue? Is she here?'

Mother Paul shook her head. 'I tried to reach you,' she told him anxiously, 'after failing to contact Inspector Savage.'

'Then she is in trouble!' Gone was Ted's customary easy grin. His mouth was hard and compressed, his eyes penetrating. 'I knew when she wasn't at the flat. Quickly, Mother Paul, what do you know?'

'Only that she might be heading into danger,' replied the nun unhappily. 'She thinks she knows where Rianne is. She called me nearly an hour ago. You must go after her at once.'

'Where has she gone?'

'I don't know,' said Mother Paul helplessly. 'She was wanting to tease me, I think. All she said was that someone was waiting in a car and that she'd be late for our meeting. Oh, yes, and that there was more than gold in the hills—you know that expression?'

'Hills?' Ted's eyes flashed.

'It means something to you? And if I tell you the name of the person who I am nearly sure is responsible for all the dreadful things that have been happening?'

'Tell me everything you know!' Ted's steady gaze never left the nun's face as she spoke swiftly and with authority. He nodded once or twice in agreement even though his eyes widened in astonishment. 'I'll have to believe everything you've told me. There's no time to explain now, but there is a chance I know where she's heading.'

'Then I'll have to trust you, too,' said Mother Paul. 'Somehow I knew all along I could.'

He gave her a quick, warm smile. 'Bob Savage warned me about you.'

'Mr Savage!' Mother Paul put a hand to her cheek. 'Where shall I say you've gone?'

Ted had stepped out of the hall. 'The Willis girl will tell you,' he called over his shoulder.

'Sandra?' exclaimed the nun in surprise. She tripped down the steps after him. 'You will bring Sue back safely, won't you?' she asked unsteadily.

Ted's face was grim as he climbed quickly into the Mercedes and, after a brief salute with one hand, circled the driveway and sped off into the darkness.

Mother Paul closed the front door and gazed thoughtfully at the faces of nuns and girls peeping from all directions. 'Would someone kindly tell Sandra Willis that I wish to see her? The rest of you may go about your usual business.'

By the time Savage arrived, Mother Paul and Sandra were sitting quietly on the uncomfortable little iron chairs with which the hall was furnished. There were signs of strain on the nun's face, while the girl looked as though she had been crying. When Savage heard what had transpired, he said: 'But that place in the hills was searched after the *Rianne May Show*. There was no sign of anyone having been there. You're sure that's where Brown had gone?'

'He told me to ask Sandra and she has confessed to telephoning the studio and telling Mr Brown about the cottage,' replied Mother Paul patiently.

'Sue Berry said that if any of us thought we knew anything that might lead to Rianne, we should ring up,' explained Sandra sullenly. 'I suddenly thought of the cottage. You see, Daddy —'

'That's enough, Sandra,' said Mother Paul gently, and turned to the inspector. 'You won't waste any more time going after Mr Brown, will you? Such a clever, brave man, but somehow I feel he may need help.'

Savage gave her a long, puzzled look, not unmixed with irritation before which she dropped her eyes meekly. 'I'll be back,' he said ominously.

Outside in his car, he picked up the radio telephone and gave curt orders for a squad car to meet him on the highway leading to the hills. As he drove off through the lighted suburbs, the frown of annoyance gradually waned and a reluctant grin dispelled the grimness round his mouth. But by the time he stopped to exchange a few words with the two policemen waiting in a car on the highway, his expression was imperturbable once more. He was pinning his hopes on a previous experience of Mother Paul and her deductions.

The police car followed him closely as they sped along with sirens blaring. Savage kept a check on his mileage indicator. He knew there was a turning somewhere that he had to find. Presently he discovered that it was little more than a cart track, rough and ungraded, which climbed steeply into a lonelier section of the hills. The two cars slackened speed as they kept close to the inside of the road away from the edge which dropped to a deep, tangled gully. Their headlights shone on the ghostly trees and the thick, overgrown bush country. Savage kept peering ahead for signposts, but the scene remained desolate and remote.

Presently he sniffed sharply and, rounding a bend, saw a faint glow through the darkness. It came from a gully, half-way up the side of a hill ahead from which the road twisted sharply. Savage proceeded to the next turn and then stopped. He got out of the car and, taking his flashlight, went to the edge of the road.

'Looks like a burnt-out car!' said one of the policemen from the other car who had joined him. 'Must have happened quite recently by the look of it. Shall I go down, sir?'

Savage played the light on the smoking wreckage deep in the undergrowth. 'Stay with it!' he said, having seen enough. 'I'm going on apiece.'

He drove more quickly, taking the bends recklessly. Somehow he couldn't get rid of that smell of burning. In fact, it seemed to be getting stronger. Then he saw the blaze up the hill on his left and his foot went down hard on the accelerator. Soon his headlights picked out a rough driveway leading upwards and he pressed his powerful car along, the overgrown bush brushing him on either side.

He came on the scene suddenly—a whole house burning furiously, the sound swamping the quiet noises of the bush. He ran the car alongside the Mercedes which was parked carelessly in some bushes with the driver's door open, as though Ted had braked quickly and leapt out.

Savage got out and cupped his hands. 'Brown! Where are you?' he called. He thought he heard a faint reply above the vicious sound of old timber in flames, and called again.

'Here! Over here!'

Then he saw two huddled figures, lying on the ground away from the glow. 'Are you all right?' asked Savage sharply, as he came up to them. 'Who's that you've got there?'

Ted was sitting on the ground cradling a limp body in his arms. 'I'm okay. It's Sue!'

The girl stirred and coughed and started feebly to struggle. 'Don't try and move, Miss Berry,' said Savage, bending over her. 'You're quite safe now.'

He straightened up easily, lifting her in his arms like a child, while Ted scrambled to his feet. 'I've got some brandy in the car. Can you make it?'

'Sure! You'll probably have to hold the bottle for me. My hands hurt like all hell.'

'You're burnt? Looks as though you were just in time. Anyone else in there?' Savage jerked his head towards the blaze.

'If there is, I'm not taking a second look now,' Ted assured him.

'But someone drove a Morris out of the drive just as I came along—missed me by inches!'

'And missed the road by several feet,' said Savage grimly. 'There's a wreck in a gully about a quarter of a mile back. Does it give you any satisfaction to know that the petrol must have exploded?'

'Very little! I take it you won't be making an arrest, after all. Do you know who was in it?'

'No,' replied Savage shortly. 'Do you?'

'Mother Paul gave me a name.' Ted's voice sounded puzzled as he told Savage what the nun had said. 'Sounds fantastic, doesn't it? I'm glad that part of the business is your affair.'

Sue, who had been placed carefully in the back of the inspector's car, heard them talking and tried to sit up. Until now she had not felt the slightest inclination to do anything except wait for the nightmare to pass. She had only a dazed recollection of how she had been rescued. The last thing she remembered clearly was the awful sound of the flames and the swirling, choking smoke as she beat frantically against the bolted door of the cottage.

'Ted!' She thought she had called his name, but it came out as a husky whisper.

But he turned at once and put his head into the car. 'I'm here, Sue. Are you feeling better?'

'Was it you who carried me out . . . out of that place? I can't think why she did it. Rianne wasn't there at all. She must be mad. She pushed me in and locked the door. Then the fire started. I was scared! Oh, Ted, I was so scared!' He leant over and put his arms round her gingerly so as not to touch the rough tweed of her coat with his hands. When she clung to him, he tried not to wince. He murmured comfortingly over her, as he had once before, when she had been in trouble. Then he became more articulate. 'Quiet, darling! Don't be scared any more. Everything's all right now. Inspector Savage is here to take us home.'

'Get in the back with her,' suggested Savage. 'We'll drive back to the boys—they're by the gully where I spotted the car—then one of them can take your car back to town.'

At first Sue tried to rouse herself. A hundred things crowded her tired mind that she knew she should tell them, but, when Ted suggested she wait until they got back to town, she gave up the attempt and thankfully allowed herself to be drawn against him again. She had never felt so helpless yet so secure in her life before, so she closed her eyes and relaxed.

At the bend in the road where the squad car was waiting, Savage stopped and spoke to the policemen. 'What is it?' asked Sue drowsily, but Ted pressed her head on his shoulder again by the simple method of resting his cheek against her hair. Soon, lulled by the motion of the car and the knowledge that she was miraculously safe, Sue fell asleep.

'She's taken quite a beating, poor kid!' Ted remarked presently to Savage. There was a note of elaborate detachment in his voice that made Savage smile. He could catch glimpses of the tableau on his back seat in the rear vision mirror.

'She's been very plucky,' he agreed. 'Does she know who you are?'

'Not yet,' Ted replied. Then he added in a burst of confidence: 'I found it damned hard deceiving her all the time, I can tell you. You don't like playing a part when—'

'When it's the girl you'd much rather be completely honest with?' suggested Savage gravely as Ted paused. 'Never mind, she'll be impressed at your unmasking.'

'I only hope so,' replied Ted, and the genuine anxiety in his voice made Savage smile again. He felt incredibly old.

Sue did not stir until the car drew up at Maryhill. 'Where are we?' she asked, disengaging herself shyly. 'Oh, Maryhill! Mother Paul! That's right. She asked us to meet here.'

The front door opened as they came up the steps. Ted handed Sue to Mother Paul, who embraced her thankfully. 'Such a naughty, headstrong child! You should never trust people who commit murders. But, of course, you weren't to know. Are you all right, dear?' She looked over her head. 'I knew I could rely on you, Mr Brown. Oh, goodness gracious! Whatever has happened to you?'

'He rescued me when the cottage was set on fire,' explained Sue and then, as she realised how burnt he was, she said, appalled: 'Oh, Ted, I had no idea! And you let me sleep! You must have been in agony.'

'Sister Euphrasia!' Mother Paul called to the portress. 'Find something for burns and bring it into the parlour. And a bowl of warm water and towels. Sue, dear, take Mr Brown along.'

Savage was stripping off his coat and gloves in the background, but his eyes had never left the nun. His expression was rather grim and did not soften when Mother Paul looked at him with some reproach. 'So you've come at last, Inspector! I am so glad to see you.'

'There is a burnt-out car in one of the gullies near the Willises' country cottage,' he said slowly. 'Containing the remains of the person who was driving it. I understand she will be identified as Mrs Eunice Hurley.'

11

The nun seemed to sway and Savage put out a swift hand. But she steadied herself by gripping the back of a chair. 'Terrible!' she said, a quiver marring the customary serenity of her face. 'Moya! Carol! And then herself.'

'I don't think she killed herself deliberately,' Savage said in gentler tones. 'She was running like a panic-stricken animal. She must have realised that she had been practically caught in the act of getting rid of Miss Berry. But why, Mother Paul? And how did you come to suspect her?'

The nun raised her head. 'Shall we go in to the others?' she suggested. 'There's just one point I must confirm with Sue. She probably realises it now.'

Sue and Ted were sitting facing each other. The girl's head was bent as she gently smoothed ointment on the hands lying palm upwards on her lap. She looked up when the nun and the inspector entered and smiled at them dazedly.

'Ted's been telling me he's not really a studio security officer at all. Actually he works for the Secret Service. Even his name isn't Brown! It seems Rianne was mixed up in some political movement in England and he was posted to watch her when she came out here. Which, of course, is why he dragged me out of that beastly Servants of Peace party Roger Petrie took me to. He's been playing a part all this time, Inspector!'

'You sound impressed, Miss Berry,' remarked Savage, eyeing Ted quizzically. 'These cloak and dagger boys have it all over us plain policemen.'

Sue blushed and gave a nervous little laugh. 'I suppose you knew all along, Inspector.'

'No, indeed. But naturally after Mother Paul queried his identity, I was instantly suspicious,' said Savage solemnly.

'There was something in his eyes as well as his height,' protested the nun meekly. 'Quite a distinctive person I felt from the start. But I assure you I had no idea precisely what he was until . . . well, never mind about that yet.'

'And there was I thinking what an excellent actor I was,' murmured Ted.

'You deceived me,' said Sue, and added contritely: 'When I remember all the patronising things I said to you!'

Ted smiled at her tenderly and dragged his eyes away with an effort. 'Once Bob knew what my real job was—and checked on my story, I might add—we decided to maintain the deception as it were. I was after information concerning Rianne May's position with the Servants of Peace—to see whether, in fact, she had come to Australia to try to start a branch over here—while he was after her would-be murderer.'

'But why should Eunice Hurley want to murder Rianne?' asked Sue in a bewildered voice. 'Did she do it for Lylah's sake, as you suggested once, Mr Savage, because of Sir Hammond's interest in Rianne?'

'May I?' interrupted Mother Paul apologetically. Savage flourished a hand thankfully. 'Sue dear, let us take it step by step, starting from this afternoon. Eunice came to see you, did she not? By any chance did you ask her to call?'

'Of course not,' replied the girl, puzzled by the nun's question. 'Why should I want to do that?'

'Never mind, just for the moment. What reason did Eunice give for coming to see you?'

Sue thought for a moment. 'No proper reason,' she answered presently. 'But Eunice was always—or seemed to be—somewhat vague and jittery. As a matter of fact, I was quite surprised to see her. But she seemed more than usually nervous and so upset about Carol's death that I thought at first she merely wanted someone to talk to.'

'What did she say about Carol?'

'She kept harping on the fact that Carol had mentioned nearly being run down before, and didn't I think that was what must have happened, and the statement in the newspapers that Carol might have been deliberately killed was a mistake?'

'And what was your reply?'

Sue glanced at the inspector. 'I told her that Lylah had put forward the same suggestion at the hospital, but that the police were still not satisfied that it was an accident. She didn't say anything more about Carol after that, but I could see she was pretty shaken. Instead, she began to talk about Lylah and the friends they had been ever since their Maryhill days, and how, even now, Lylah sometimes liked to tease her by pretending to become more interested in someone else — just as she used to at school.

'It all sounded rather silly to me, so I said maybe it would be better if Eunice wasn't so much with Lylah, learnt to stand on her own two feet, then she wouldn't be so hurt by what Lylah did. I also had in mind that if Lylah didn't have anyone to lend an ear to her grievances and constantly building up her ego, she might do something to improve her relations with her husband.'

'Did you mention this to Eunice?' asked Mother Paul.

Sue smiled ruefully. 'She didn't give me the chance. She burst into a flood of tears and began accusing me of turning Lylah against her — just as Moya had! From what I could make out, Lylah's appointing me treasurer of the Association was the crux of the trouble.'

Mother Paul leant forward. 'Ah!' she exclaimed softly, but filling the word with barely suppressed excitement.

'As far as I was concerned,' Sue went on unthinkingly, 'Eunice was welcome to the job. I'd been working on a balance sheet for hours when she arrived. I was stuck because —' she broke off and stared at Mother Paul.

The nun nodded encouragingly. 'Go on, dear.'

'The figures were several hundred pounds out,' Sue continued more slowly, 'which I traced to discrepancies in the two trust funds established by the Association. At first I thought perhaps Moya hadn't accounted for them properly and I had already decided that she'd been pretty hopeless at the job of treasurer. It seemed to me that only Lylah Willis would be able to explain about the trust funds, because she was the only one left who had authority to sign cheques. Both Moya and Carol were dead and . . . ' her voice dwindled away and her eyes widened.

'I wondered if it was in connection with the accounts that you had perhaps asked Eunice to call,' explained the nun. 'Did you happen to mention the matter to her at all?'

'Yes. I tried to tell her about the accounts, hoping the change of subject would take her mind off her trouble. In fact, I was in the middle of telling her all about it when she suddenly jumped up and, out of the blue, announced that she knew where Rianne was and that she would take me to her. Naturally I lost all interest in accounts and balance sheets then.'

'Oh, Sue! Sue!' Mother Paul shook her head.

Suddenly Sue understood. Moya had been treasurer, Carol assistant treasurer. 'You . . . you mean, that was Eunice's motive? That was why she called? Because she had been taking money from the trust funds and realised I might find the discrepancy and begin to put two and two together? But then what about Rianne?'

'Just a minute, Miss Berry!' Savage broke in crisply. 'Mother Paul, are you suggesting that Rianne May wasn't the intended victim, after all? That Mrs Hurley killed Moya Curran because she was going to denounce her at the reunion for misappropriation of funds?'

The nun met his stern look. 'That was partly the reason—perhaps the final incentive. But the motive went deeper than that.'

'Then perhaps you will be good enough to enlighten us,' requested the inspector grimly.

'I'll be glad to,' admitted Mother Paul meekly. 'The whole structure of Eunice Hurley's life, which she had for years been carefully building up around her rich and powerful friend, Lady Willis, was in jeopardy. There was not only herself to consider, but she had also involved her daughter's welfare. Jillian was to benefit from her friendship with Sandra Willis, just as Eunice had fastened herself on Sandra's mother. Whenever Lylah showed favouritism to another, Eunice went through an agony of jealousy and apprehension. But until Moya came along, she was always able to beat the spectre of being cast aside.

'But Moya was different. Not only had she gained what might seem to others the doubtful privilege of Lylah's patronage, but she had also stumbled on to something that would destroy any claims Eunice might have on her friend. If Lylah learnt that Eunice had been stealing money from the funds of one of her pet organisations—and I think we'll find that she had been deriving a neat income from them for some years now—then Eunice would be tipped out of her well-feathered nest. Which must never happen. As Eunice looked on Moya as a rival, it did not seem likely to her that she'd be able to persuade her to keep quiet about the missing funds. There was only one thing to do, therefore, and that was to remove Moya.'

'And Miss Frazer?' enquired Savage in a tight voice. 'Was she another rival to be removed?'

'No, indeed!' replied Mother Paul with some asperity, as though dealing with a deliberately obtuse pupil. 'But from what Janet Gordon told me this morning on the telephone about the conversation between you all at the hospital last night, it was obvious to me that Carol must also have come to realise that the trust funds had been tampered with. Perhaps she noticed something when she was packing up her Maryhill books to give them to Sue—just as I did, as I will explain presently. But I doubt if she thought of Eunice in connection with the discrepancies: she probably thought Lylah Willis the culprit. Sue was to do the same. Am I not right, dear?'

'Because Carol knew that all cheques needed Lylah's signature,' agreed Sue. 'I can't understand that unless . . . unless . . . '

'Go on,' nodded Mother Paul again.

Sue frowned in concentration. 'Eunice was always with Lylah, cadging everything she could—clothes, the use of one of the Willis's cars, even a friend for her daughter! She made herself indispensable to Lylah by listening to her marital problems and her charity speeches and doing little odds and ends of jobs, like making her phone calls and writing her letters and . . . and perhaps signing Lylah's name to them?'

The silence that followed was broken by Savage, whose voice held a faintly grudging note of admiration: 'That could well be the explanation. It won't be difficult to check now that we suspect forgery. Naturally a bank would not think to question the signature of the wife of a near-millionaire, especially as Eunice had no doubt perfected Lady Willis's signature. But whatever made you think Mrs Hurley would know where Rianne was, Miss Berry?'

Sue hesitated. 'Well, you seemed to suspect Sir Hammond was hiding her,' she replied, trying to imitate some of Mother Paul's meek demeanour. 'When Eunice mentioned the cottage in the hills as belonging to him, I didn't doubt that Rianne would be there. I thought Eunice must have seen or overheard something.'

'Providence must have inspired you to ring me,' exclaimed Mother Paul impulsively, gladly forgetting that it had been pure high spirits. 'I was quite in despair at first, as I knew you were being deliberately misled.'

'Yes, you were quite sure it was a trap,' agreed Ted, sounding puzzled.

'All the way to the hills in the car she had borrowed from Lylah,' went on Sue, 'Eunice kept talking about her. I realise now that, after my mentioning about the trust funds, she was afraid I might stumble on to the truth and was trying to divert suspicion. It had already occurred to me as odd that a wealthy woman like Lylah should need to steal.

'Before I got into the car I noticed one of the mudguards was badly dented. Eunice was a shocking driver, careering all over the road and making a nuisance of herself generally. I mentioned the dent, hoping she'd steady down. She said quickly that Lylah must have caused it. Then she let me know in a roundabout fashion that Lylah was without an alibi at the time of Carol's accident; that she, Eunice, didn't arrive at the Willis's place until much later than Lylah led us to believe, Inspector.'

'I thought last night that Sir Hammond volunteered his wife's alibi a bit too smoothly,' admitted Savage. 'I wouldn't be surprised if each of them was concerned about the other knowing more than they would admit.'

'Then the person Sir Hammond found Carol Frazer telephoning when he called on her could have been Mrs Hurley?' suggested Ted, coming into the discussion again. He had all this time been regarding Mother Paul with frank incredulity.

Savage nodded. 'If — as Mother Paul considers likely — Carol had not got beyond the point of suspecting Lady Willis responsible for the tampered funds, then that telephone conversation, her strange manner towards Sir Hammond and young Bexhill's story concerning her references to Miss Berry being in trouble, all make sense.'

'And Mrs Hurley—realising that a quick-witted girl like Carol would soon get to the truth despite her first assumption that her step-sister was guilty—decided to get rid of her at once?'

Mother Paul nodded, and then spoke with great sadness: 'It is my honest opinion that, but for certain means which she had and the opportunity to hand, Eunice would never have started her wicked plan to kill poor Moya. But having embarked on it, she found—as murderers always do—that she either had to kill again or else be found out. She probably thought that, once she was rid of Moya, all would be well as regards the niche she had made for herself with Lylah. She hoped, no doubt, that Lylah would ask her to take on the accounts along with her other duties when she would be able to cover up. But Sue appeared on the scene and again she felt faced with a rival. And exposure!'

'Perhaps,' remarked Savage in more kindly tones, 'when she went to see Miss Berry, it was with the hope that she'd be able to get the Maryhill books from her. But Miss Berry, like Carol, was already on the way to knowing too much. So Eunice put into operation the plan with which she had gone armed—pretending to know where Rianne May was so as to lure Miss Berry to an out-of-the-way spot. The second and third murders were made to look like accidents—a hit and run driver and an old weatherboard country cottage that is the classic fire risk.'

Remembering the horror of that burning cottage, Sue shivered and Ted covered her hand with his bandaged one.

'When did you come to suspect that Rianne May was not the intended victim?' Savage asked Mother Paul curiously.

The nun pondered for a moment. 'Lylah gave me instructions to hand to Sue all Moya's papers which were left behind in the confusion following her murder. Perhaps it wasn't any of my business but I looked through them and could find neither the treasurer's report nor the balance sheet. So odd for a general meeting, I thought, and I had a distinct recollection of poor Moya studying them so earnestly. Of course Eunice had to hope that their absence wouldn't be considered remarkable after all the disturbance. But the more I thought, the more I wondered how they could have been mislaid. I knew you hadn't taken anything, Inspector.

'I decided finally to phone Lylah to tell her someone must have taken them. Then suddenly it occurred to me what an odd thing it was to do in the middle of a murder—take away accounts. . . The only way the loss didn't seem strange was to contemplate it as the reason for the murder. In which case, it seemed obvious that Moya *could* have been the intended victim since she had prepared the balance sheet and its covering report. Eunice gave herself away there. In acting the distressed and not over-intelligent witness—though I daresay she was horrified to see the result of her action—she rather drew attention when Lylah said there would be no meeting that day by declaring that Moya was the only one who would have understood the balance sheet.'

Savage smiled, albeit rather crookedly. 'Would you have told me all this had I come to see you earlier?'

'Indeed, yes,' she assured him earnestly. 'I wanted Sue to explain to you that I wasn't willingly withholding information from you. There were several matters I wanted your advice about. Just odd little things, and though they seemed to fit in with Rianne's being the intended victim, they could also have been applied to Moya. For example, the talk about Moya having been distressed about something before the meeting. Lylah brought that up, if you remember, Sue? Moya had told her that she was in for a shock, something for which Moya considered herself partly to blame. It is quite clear now that Moya was referring to her intention of revealing the state of the trust funds. Whether she knew Eunice was to blame, I cannot decide. But Eunice most certainly must have known of the report and what the balance sheet showed. Do you remember Eunice attributing Moya's words to Rianne's imminent arrival at the reunion, Sue?'

'Lylah was making herself so unpopular that no one was heeding her,' agreed Sue. 'Just as we didn't heed her last night when she said Carol had declared she had been nearly run over before. But Eunice had remembered what Carol said and used it as a plan to get rid of her.'

'Then there was the fact that Eunice deliberately connived to have Rianne attend the reunion. Admittedly all the girls, except Lylah, agreed to invite her but it was, I think, Eunice who ensured her coming. Am I not right, Sue?'

'You mean because Eunice rang me asking if I could prevent Rianne's accepting the invitation? When Rianne heard she was not wanted because of Lylah, she naturally made a point of attending.'

'Exactly!' said Mother Paul. 'Rianne had to be at that reunion for Eunice's plans to be successful—to divert suspicion which must instantly have fallen on someone at the tea-table. It had to appear that Rianne was the intended victim.'

'Are you saying it was Mrs Hurley who sent those anonymous letters to Rianne May?' demanded Savage incredulously.

'I think so,' replied the nun. 'How else was she to make it appear that only chance was to blame for a murder at Maryhill? Rianne's life had to be already threatened. According to what Sue told us of the conversation at the table, it was common knowledge that Rianne followed a diet which included the use of saccharine tablets in the place of sugar. Eunice had only to see to it that there was no sugar bowl and there was a good chance of Rianne's offering her tablets around. Even had she not done so, there were still Lylah and Carol and perhaps Janet to fall back on as scapegoats.'

'Then how was the poison actually administered?'

'I can only guess,' said Mother Paul apologetically. 'Probably in one of those delightful little almond cakes that Sister Martha never fails to make each year for the reunion. Eunice had only to make one similar to Sister Martha's and see that it was on the cake-stand closest to Moya—but that is just supposition.'

'I can't see how you can fail to be wrong now,' remarked Ted, who had been regarding the nun with wholehearted admiration.

'Mind you,' Mother Paul went on, 'if we had taken notice of what Janet said, we would soon have realised that the poison wasn't put into Moya's tea at all, and that the murderer was close at hand and not just anyone in a wide field of suspects. Janet still insists that there was no smell of cyanide in Moya's cup which she picked up at once. Yet your men found traces in the cup later, did they not, Mr Savage? Therefore someone must have put poison into a cup during the confusion so as to make it look as though Moya had taken a poisoned tablet intended for Rianne.

'It was that fact, along with the missing balance sheet, that convinced me that the murderer was one of the girls. Think now, Sue!'

Mother Paul turned to the girl. 'You were there. What did you see?'

Sue thought for several minutes and then replied slowly: 'I saw Eunice pick up the bowl of flowers that had been spilt, and then dab at the cloth with her handkerchief.'

'Doesn't it usually happen that a person's reaction to knocking anything over is to right the object? When Moya became ill and you all got up to crane over the table to see what was the matter, Eunice quickly reached across for the balance sheet and report. Only someone stretching across the table could have upset the bowl. Then she started to mop up the mess with her handkerchief, under cover of which she hastily put the remains of the cyanide capsule into the nearest cup, knowing it would be found sooner or later.'

'Cyanide capsule!' echoed Savage. 'But where on earth did she get that?'

Mother Paul regarded him apologetically. 'I'm rather inclined to think from that poor crazy man,' she replied simply.

'What crazy . . .? You don't mean that fellow who broke in here the other night! The patient from the psychiatric ward at Wesburn Hospital?'

The nun inclined her head. 'That's what I meant about Eunice having already the means in her possession. And Rianne's presence provided her opportunity.'

'Wesburn!' said Sue on an exasperated breath. 'Do you know Eunice actually mentioned that hospital the day she rang me, pretending to put Rianne off from going to the reunion? She was reciting a list of Lylah's charitable activities, trying to impress upon me what a wonderful woman Lylah was. Of course she trotted round to these places with Lylah. How did I get the impression, though, that the poor man was after Rianne that night?'

'Do you recall the newspapers the day after the reunion?' asked Mother Paul. 'The man probably saw them, too, and it set him thinking. There was a picture of Rianne looking perfectly lovely. And one of Moya and also a very good one of Lylah in her Red Cross uniform.'

'Then it was Lylah he was looking for?'

'Not Lylah herself, but the friend who was always with her on her visits round the wards at Wesburn Hospital. Don't you recall his asking you if you were her friend—meaning Lylah's friend—and you took it he meant Rianne? I believe he gave Eunice his cyanide capsule one day, thinking she was a nurse or someone official because of the uniform. That male attendant who collected the poor fellow remarked on how he always gave up harmful objects when he felt, what he termed, "a bout" coming on.'

'But how would he happen to have a cyanide capsule?' demanded Savage.

'Either he had kept it secret for years, or perhaps he had managed to steal it at the hospital. If he had harmful objects to give up, then he must have gathered them from somewhere.'

'He had been in the Korean War,' said Savage thoughtfully. 'His mental condition was due to having been captured and tortured by the Communists.'

'So we gathered from his rather odd and unhappy discourse,' said the nun. 'I made further enquiries about him through the hospital chaplain. And from what that dear man left unsaid and the austere way he gave me a lecture on the immorality of suicide under any conditions, I was led to understand that our unfortunate visitor had had something to do with Intelligence and could have been issued with cyanide in case of capture.'

'And he came looking for the woman to whom he had given the poison so that she wouldn't attempt further harm against Rianne?' asked Sue. 'Rianne, who was the ward's pin-up girl!'

'I think the poor man in his clouded mind knew what had happened, but having got as far as Maryhill his thought processes just broke down. But I feel sure, Inspector, that if you should question him gently in some of his more lucid moments, you might find what he has to say of interest, though perhaps not reliable evidence. Shall I go on?'

'Please do!' said Savage who was taking notes.

'The second anonymous letter was further proof that the poisoner must have been at Maryhill. The purpose in sending it was to stress that Rianne was the intended victim. But the letter must have been posted on Sunday evening before either the news of the tragedy or Rianne's disappearance were released. Rumour could have spread regarding the murder but certainly not about Rianne's running away. Only someone who had been present at Maryhill, yet was unaware of Rianne's disappearance, could have prepared it. From what Sue told me about it, I got the impression that it had been made up in advance along with the first letter—which is what Eunice did, knowing she was going to send it, anyway. It was all part of the plan to take the murderer away from Maryhill, to make it seem as if the poison capsule had been put into the saccharine bottle.'

'And Eunice didn't know about Rianne's disappearance because, when she rang, Inspector Savage made signs to me not to mention it,' declared Sue. 'Perhaps she was checking on what was happening before she posted it? Sir Hammond was concerned about that second letter, too. I think he was worried about Lylah having something to do with it.'

'Then Rianne's position in the case was only to create an illusion,' observed Ted. His eyes twinkled suddenly. 'She wouldn't like that.'

'Why, Mother Paul!' exclaimed Sue excitedly. 'You said something like that when we were watching the *Rianne May Show* in the recreation room, and then later to Janet Gordon. You knew what was real and what was phoney even then!'

'In a way, dear. When you informed me that the studio was not as large or as glamorous as it appeared on camera, I was struck by a parallel: what actually happened and what the murderer wanted us to see.'

'But Rianne?' persisted Sue. 'Did she run away or has someone been forcing her to remain hidden?'

Mother Paul turned to Ted. 'This subversive movement that Rianne became involved with in England, were they putting some pressure on her to help extend their activities here?'

He nodded and grew serious. 'Rianne thought, when she came to Australia, that she was leaving those troubles behind her. But she soon learned that disassociating herself from them wasn't so easy. The movement has need of big names and influential members. She was a very frightened woman about the whole business, imagining she was so deeply implicated that there was no way out of her predicament. Actually, she has only to come to us and we will be glad to help—and glad to have information she has concerning the movement.'

'I realise now why she kept putting Roger Petrie off,' said Sue. 'But what about Greg? Did she think he had something to do with the movement?'

'Rianne had been told that someone would contact her,' said Ted. 'Roger Petrie did not approach her at first, so she tried to find out where the trouble spot lay. She may have had some plan to fight the influence of the movement. I couldn't find out much from just watching her and I didn't want to arouse either her suspicions or alarm her by too many questions. That was when she started on Greg Oliphant—she thought he might be the contact. Bob told me about the interview he had with him.'

'She's not really in trouble then, is she?' asked Sue, in a worried voice. 'In some ways, Rianne isn't very bright, you know. I tried to explain that to Mother Paul once. She is very childlike in her fears and enthusiasms.'

'Then no one would be surprised if it were found that Rianne thought the anonymous letter Eunice sent came instead from the people who were putting pressure on her,' suggested Mother Paul casually. 'Or that she ran literally for her life—so she thought—following Moya's murder.'

'Do you think Eric Watts has been concealing her all this time?' Sue asked Savage. 'After all, she did go through a form of marriage with him years ago.'

'If he has, then he's been pretty clever about it,' replied Savage. 'I've had a man detailed to watch his movements. I'm inclined to think Mr Watt's interest in his one-time wife is purely mercenary.'

'I suppose,' said Sue tentatively, 'when you have verified Mother Paul's story, Inspector, you'll make some sort of statement and Rianne will come out of hiding. Unless,' the girl turned to Ted, 'those awful Servants of Peace people have been keeping her prisoner?'

He smiled at her worried face comfortingly. 'They wouldn't dare! I think, in any case, it will only be a matter of time before they're disbanded.'

'Then where is Rianne?' demanded Sue, in a bewildered voice.

'That is a mystery even Mother Paul has not attempted to solve,' said Savage, with a rueful smile.

The nun, who had been silent, looking from one to the other, suddenly appeared somewhat sheepish. 'Well, to tell you the truth,' she confessed humbly, 'I can solve it.'

Three pairs of eyes stared at her uncomprehendingly.

'Rianne is here,' the soft voice confessed.

Still the three pairs of eyes stared.

'Yes, truly she is!' Mother Paul assured them earnestly. 'She's been at Maryhill all the time, in Father Maher's little house in our grounds. Poor Father! Every night he had to go over to the local presbytery. He will be so relieved to have his house to himself once more—though he and Rianne used to play cards together and talk by the hour. I do hope he managed to straighten out her marital affairs—such a disagreeable creature Mr Watts sounds! Though I daresay Rianne herself was—'

Ted found his voice first: 'So that is why you were so sure Sue was walking into a trap!'

'Rianne May was here all the time—and you didn't inform me!' exclaimed Savage, after swallowing hard.

'Oh, please don't look so stern!' the nun begged. 'Didn't I keep asking you to come and see me? Such a position I was in! Rianne had made me promise not to tell anyone where she was. She was in a shocking state of distress when I found her in the garden not long after you and Sue had left. She'd walked all the way from her flat after deciding that she had no one else to turn to but me. Such an odd coincidence, Sue! She said precisely what you said—that she wished she were back at Maryhill. Safe.'

'Rianne May was here!' repeated Savage, obviously scarcely able to credit his own ears.

'She was nearly out of her mind with fear over that horrid movement,' explained Mother Paul quickly. 'At that time, of course, I had no idea what everything was about, so I hurried her through the pine grove to the Priest's House. She was so distraught that it was impossible to talk to her then, so I went back to the main house to make some tea.

'Poor Sister Martha! She must have wondered many times these last few days who has been robbing the larder. The occasions I've had to wait until her back was turned! Sue, dear! The bell in the corner! We arranged it as a signal. Dear Rianne does so love to make an entrance!'

Sue got up and moved across the room as in a dream. Presently there was a sound of swift footsteps crossing the parquet hall, then the door was flung open and Rianne May made the most spectacular entrance of her career.

With a choking cry, Sue rushed forward.

'Why, Sue!' Rianne's enchanting laugh rang out. 'Darling, how wonderful to see you! Have you been worried about me? And my faithful old Ted!' She ran to him and kissed him on the cheek. 'Mother Paul and I have been working out such stories about you. Why didn't you tell me who you were? So thrilling! My dears, don't look too closely at me. I'm a positive fright! No make-up and the same clothes for days. And who is this handsome he-man type?'

Savage had risen and was observing Rianne with an expression which was half-amused and half-exasperated. Sue introduced him and then moved close to Ted. She felt lost when she was not near him now. He gave her a long, smiling look, as though he could not wait to kiss her.

Savage took the hand Rianne held out to him in queenly style. 'You've given us quite a deal of trouble, Miss May,' he began.

'Oh, please don't scold—not yet, anyway,' said Rianne coaxingly. 'Mother Paul says I've got nothing to worry about and that you're a terribly nice person. Let me plan my return to the world first. Sue, get hold of Hammond and tell him where I am. Then the newspapers—no, wait! We'd better go to the flat so that I can tizzy up. Ring Make-up to send a girl along—my hair's in a mess. Now about clothes . . .'

Mother Paul drew Savage away. 'Quite useless!' she told him, with a sympathetic twinkle. 'Just like a child, as Sue pointed out. And after all the publicity and the sensation of her return she'll be too busy preparing for another special edition of the *Rianne May Show*.'

'Which I will make a point of not watching,' said Inspector Savage forthrightly. 'Well, I suppose it doesn't really matter. You've told me all I want to know. I apologise for my initial scepticism. Would you allow me to express my great appreciation—and admiration?'

'No, please don't,' requested the nun quietly. 'It has not been a happy time—except perhaps for Sue and that nice boy I hope she means to marry. I'll be glad to get away from Maryhill.'

'What?' demanded Savage, disappointed. 'You're being moved on?'

'My term of office will be up at the end of the year. It doesn't do for us to become attached to one place. I don't know where I will be sent next.'

There was a pause. Then Savage said gravely: 'No doubt I will learn of your whereabouts one day. When a message is put on my desk that the Reverend Mother Mary St. Paul of the Cross requests my *immediate* attendance, I shall know what to expect.'

THE END

MORE BOOKS BY JUNE WRIGHT

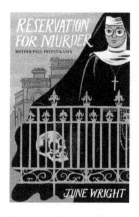

RESERVATION FOR MURDER

June Wright had already published several highly praised mysteries before she created her most memorable detective, the Reverend Mother Mary St Paul of the Cross. Mother Paul may seem distracted or absent-minded, but nothing important escapes her attention—she turns out to have a shrewd grasp of everything that's going on beneath the surface of events. In the first of her three mysteries featuring this unlikely and endearing heroine, the kindly nun is in charge of a residential hostel for young working women in Melbourne. Several of them have received nasty anonymous letters, and an atmosphere of suspicion and accusation has spread throughout the house. When Mary Allen finds a stranger stabbed to death in the garden, and a few days later one of the residents is found drowned, an apparent suicide, the tension reaches fever pitch. Is there a connection between the two deaths? Or between them and the poison-pen letters? The police investigation, abetted by the resourceful Mary Allen, proceeds in fits and starts, but meanwhile Mother Paul pursues her own enquiries. With an introduction by Derham Groves and a special bonus: the short story "Mother Paul Investigates," which marked the first appearance in print of the nun detective.

FACULTY OF MURDER

Mother Paul, returns to her sleuthing ways in her new position as warden of a student hall of residence at the University of Melbourne. No sooner has Judith Mornane arrived on campus than she startles her fellow residents by announcing her intention to discover the murderer of her sister, who disappeared without trace from the same dorm a year earlier. The ever-curious Mother Paul is drawn to investigate—did Judith's sister simply run off for reasons best known to herself, as the police concluded, or could it be she really was murdered? Could her disappearance be linked to a campus tragedy at around the same time—the bathtub drowning of a college professor's wife? And that drowning—was it as accidental as the official investigation suggested?

Mother Paul believes the events must be connected, and a further death, this time of one of her student charges, convinces her a particularly cruel and clever murderer is still at work within the college. The Reverend Mother is not above a little subterfuge in the interests of discovering the truth, and she moves her colleagues, the students, and even the police around like so many figures on a chessboard until finally, amid high drama, the murderer is revealed. With an introduction by Lucy Sussex.

MORE BOOKS BY JUNE WRIGHT

MURDER IN THE TELEPHONE EXCHANGE

When *Murder in the Telephone Exchange* was reissued in 2014, June Wright was hailed by the *Sydney Morning Herald* as "our very own Agatha Christie," and a new generation of readers fell in love with her blend of intrigue and psychological suspense—and with her winning heroine, Maggie Byrnes.

When an unpopular colleague at Melbourne Central is murdered, Maggie resolves to turn sleuth. Some of her co-workers are acting strangely, and Maggie is convinced she has a better chance of figuring out the killer's identity than the stodgy police team assigned to the case, who seem to think she herself might have had something to do with it. But then one of her friends is murdered too, and it looks like Maggie is next in line.

This is a mystery in the tradition of Dorothy L. Sayers, full of verve and wit. It also offers an evocative account of Melbourne in the early postwar years, as young women flocked to the big city, leaving behind small-town life for jobs, boarding houses and independence. Featuring an extended biographical introduction by Derham Groves.

SO BAD A DEATH

Maggie Byrnes, the heroine of *Murder in the Telephone Exchange*, returns to the fray in *So Bad a Death*. She is now married and living in a Melbourne suburb, but violent death nevertheless dogs her footsteps even in apparently tranquil Middleburn.

It's no great surprise when a widely disliked local bigwig (who happens to be her landlord) is shot, but Maggie suspects someone is also targeting the infant who is his heir. Her compulsion to investigate puts everyone she loves in danger.

This edition includes the wonderful Gothic illustrations by Frank Whitmore that accompanied *So Bad a Death* when it was serialized in *Woman's Day* magazine in 1949, prior to its publication in book form. With an introduction by Lucy Sussex, plus an extended and revealing interview with June Wright that Lucy Sussex conducted with June Wright in 1996.

MORE BOOKS BY JUNE WRIGHT

DUCK SEASON DEATH

June Wright wrote this lost gem in the mid-1950s, but consigned it to her bottom drawer after her publisher foolishly rejected it. Perhaps it was simply ahead of its time, because while it delivers a bravura twist on the classic 'country house' murder mystery, it's also a sharp-eyed and sparkling send-up of the genre.

When someone takes advantage of a duck hunt to murder publisher Athol Sefton at a remote hunting inn, it soon turns out that almost everyone, guests and staff alike, had good reason to shoot him. Sefton's nephew Charles believes he can solve the crime by applying the traditional "rules of the game" he's absorbed over years as a reviewer of detective fiction. Much to his annoyance, however, the killer doesn't seem to be playing by those rules, and Charles finds that he is the one under suspicion. *Duck Season Death* is a both a devilishly clever whodunit and a delightful entertainment.

THE DEVIL'S CARESS

A classic country-house mystery with an emotional intensity worthy of Daphne du Maurier. Overworked young medic Marsh Mowbray has been invited to the weekend home of her revered mentor, Dr. Kate Waring, on the wild southern coast of the Mornington Peninsula outside Melbourne. Marsh is hoping to get some much-needed rest, but her stay turns out to be anything but relaxing. As storms rage outside, the house on the cliff's edge seethes with hatred and tension. Two suspicious deaths follow in quick succession, and there is no shortage of suspects. "Doubt is the devil's caress,", one of the characters tells Marsh, as her resolute efforts to get to the bottom of the deaths force her to question everyone's motives, including those of Dr. Kate.